Ellen ꭒꭒꭒ ꭒꭒꭒꭒꭒꭒꭒꭒꭒ ꭒꭒ ꭒꭒ

of two anthologies: *Bad Girls: 26 Writers Misbehave* and *Dirty Words: a Literary Encyclopaedia of Sex*. She lived in Paris for five years and now lives in the San Francisco Bay Area with her husband. She has two daughters. Ellen has worked as a tennis instructor, restaurant manager, and teacher but through all the transmutations of her life she has been writing, since the age of six, stubbornly, persistently, with great cockiness and wild insecurity, through praise and piles of rejection letters. She has given up her writing career many times, but only for a day or two, and her family has now learned to ignore her new career choices.

www.ellensussman.com

French Lessons

ELLEN SUSSMAN

Constable & Robinson Ltd
55–56 Russell Square
London WC1B 4HP
www.constablerobinson.com

First published in the US by Ballantine,
an imprint of the Random House Publishing Group, 2011
First published in the UK by Corsair,
an imprint of Constable & Robinson, 2011

Copyright © Ellen Sussman, 2011

This edition published by Canvas,
an imprint of Constable & Robinson, 2012

A copy of the British Library Cataloguing in Publication
Data is available from the British Library

ISBN: 978-1-78033-384-7

1 3 5 7 9 10 8 6 4 2

For Gillian and Sophie, my Parisian girls,
and for Neal, mon amour

FRENCH LESSONS

The Tutors

quatorze ans déj[à]
à Paris et que vou[s]
si souvent à votre
[m]ère ; Germaine es[t]
aujourd'hui, qu'ell[e]
[b]ien petite alors
[u]n cependant, rép[ond]
dan Tonvenin, à
[ré]alité appréciable
[je] te prie combien
[in]téressants à san[s]
[m]oins formons pa[s]

*B*rilliant sunlight spills through the windows of the Vivre à la Française language school. It has been raining for days—for weeks—and the sudden flash of sun through a break in the clouds causes everyone in the dreary office to stop for a moment and turn their faces toward the light. It's early morning and no one is quite awake—one young woman murmurs, *"Bonjour, soleil."* Nico smiles. Then the door slams and everyone stirs, suddenly alert. Nico blinks and looks around, hoping for a sign of what he already knows: Something's different. It's not just the sun. It's the day, new and promising. Every corner of the office looks sun-washed and bright. Even the ghostly girl behind the desk offers Nico a half smile when she hands him his daily work sheet.

Sure enough, today's teaching assignment promises something new—Josie Felton. He likes the name. It's so very American, and he imagines a blond, ponytailed girl, ready to conquer Paris. *His* Paris. He'll show her the way. He tucks the computer printout with her name and the details of their lesson—meeting time, duration, level of French, areas of concentration—into his back pocket.

It's time to meet Chantal at the café.

Nico walks out of the language school onto rue de Paradis. Before he turns to the corner restaurant, he looks down the street in the other direction. Something has caught his attention—a gasp, the rustle of fabric, a bare arm. He squints in the sun and sees two people at the end of the street. A woman pushes a man up against the wall of the building. Her arms, bare and tattooed, a lightning flash zigzagging across tan flesh, pin the man's shoulders. She leans in for a kiss that takes a long time. Someone pushes through the door behind Nico and bumps into him.

"Sorry," he says and steps aside.

Nico looks back. The woman saunters away. The man runs his hand through his hair and walks toward Nico. It's Philippe. Nico's first thought is of Chantal—did she see the kiss? He looks toward the café and Chantal is there, sitting at a table outside, reading a book. Nico takes a breath.

Philippe reaches him in a second and smacks his arm.

"I'm late, man," Philippe says in French. "Order me an espresso."

"Got it," Nico says.

Philippe heads into the language school and the door swings closed behind him.

Nico, Philippe, and Chantal have coffee together on Monday and Friday mornings after they get their assignments at the school. There are other French instructors—who teach regular classes rather than individual sessions, mostly older men and women who seem to have nothing in common with these three—though sometimes Nico wonders what he has in common with Philippe. Maybe they only really share one thing: an attraction to Chantal.

Nico hurries to the café. He can see the curve of Chantal's neck as she peers at her novel, her umbrella perched at her side, her cardigan neatly buttoned. He thinks of her in bed last week, after they made love, her hair fanned across the pillow, her body beaded with sweat, her features soft. A different person. He wants both of them.

He leans over and gives her a kiss on each cheek, then slides into the chair next to her. He smells her perfume, something that reminds him of the Mediterranean, and he has the odd sensation of stepping into the cool water of the sea. He looks around—the café is crowded and noisy—and every conversation seems too loud and hurried. A man shouts at the driver of a car who blasts his horn in response. Nico imagines a different café, somewhere in Provence. Let's drive to the sea, he would say.

He can feel the heat of the newly hatched sun on his back. Chantal tilts her head and looks at him as if she wants to read his thoughts. When they made love she pulled him onto her, so that all the space between them disappeared. Now he feels the need to touch her. First her mouth, where there is a hint of a smile. Her lips are full and he sees that she has worn lipstick. Does she always wear lipstick?

"Philippe is late," he says in French. "He'll be here soon."

"Of course," she says.

"Do you have your American again?" he asks.

"The last day," she tells Nico. "I'm a little sad about it."

"He's stolen your heart?"

She shakes her head. "He hasn't tried."

"And if he tried?"

"He's a happily married man," she says. "There aren't many of them. It's good to find one once in a while."

Nico imagines Chantal next to him in a convertible, like a young Catherine Deneuve, a scarf around her hair, the sea stretching along the coast, the road twisting through green hills, the air full of the smell of lavender.

The waiter appears. He's young, bored, and reeks of last night's booze. Nico wants to tell the kid to go home and take a shower. When he looks around the café, he realizes that most of the customers are younger than he is. He's thirty-two years old—when did he become an old guy? Nico orders a *café crème* and an espresso for Philippe. When the waiter leaves, Nico waves the stale air away.

"And you?" Chantal asks. "Who do you have today?"

"A woman. I don't know if she's young or old. Also American. High level of French."

"Lucky you."

"Apparently she's a high school French teacher. Why would a French teacher need a tutor for a day?"

"You'll find out soon enough."

Chantal tucks her hair behind her ears. She, too, looks older than the girls who flutter in their chairs, texting on cell phones, giggling with their friends. Nico hears the high-pitched voice of one girl—*"Mais non, c'est pas possible!"*—and the girl swats at a boy's face. The boy leans forward and brushes his thumb across the girl's lips. Nico pulls his eyes away. He looks at Chantal, who sips her espresso. She is twenty-eight. She is a woman compared to these girls. Again, he wants to touch her. He looks at her fingers resting on the table. She wears a simple silver ring, something that could be mistaken for a wedding band.

He reaches for her hand and pulls it closer to him. The band has something etched on it. Finally he sees that it's a vine, encircling her finger.

"I like that," he tells her.

"It's a broken promise," she says.

He waits for her to explain, feeling the heat of her hand in his.

"Philippe gave it to me," she tells him, and her hand drifts away.

Nico looks across the street. Still no sign of Philippe.

"I have news," he says. He wants to tell her before Philippe comes. He leans forward, ready to share his secret. He has told no one. "I sold my poetry collection yesterday!"

"Bravo!" Chantal says, her eyes wide. "And I didn't even know you were a poet!"

"I don't tell many people." In fact, he has only confessed his creative aspirations to his parents, who complained that he should give it up and devote himself to a real career. And so he didn't share the news with them last night. Besides, he's not sure how they'll react to the poems when they finally read them.

"What do you write about?" Chantal asks. Her face lights up—this is the Chantal he fell for weeks ago, the woman who listened to him tell a long story about his first girlfriend in Normandy and who asked him, with so much kindness, "Will you always love her best?" "No," he had told her, "I hope not." He did not say: Maybe I will love you best.

"It's a series of poems that are all about the same story. A boy is kidnapped from his home. He's gone for twenty-four hours. Each poem is a different version of what happens to him in those twenty-four hours."

"Who was kidnapped?" Philippe asks, dropping into a seat at their small, round table. He sets his messenger bag on the ground beside his chair.

Nico feels a tightening of his chest—he has lost the chance to tell her more.

"Were you kidnapped?" Chantal asks.

"It's just something I wrote," Nico says. Another time, he'll show Chantal the poems. He'll tell her the story of his day in the root cellar. In a quick moment, he feels the terror that he has lived with for so long. He's a child standing on the top of a tower of wooden wine boxes. The air smells of earth and potatoes and wine. He peers through the gap in the top of the hatch and can see the legs of policemen, dozens of policemen, their black boots stomping through wet mud. Even now, years later, he's not sure whether he's more scared that they'll find him or never find him.

He hasn't told anyone about that day. Now he's written thirty poems, inventing and reinventing that single experience of his childhood. Last night on the phone the editor told him, "This book will be a gift to us all. The rest of us have our childhood experiences. You have your childhood experience and your bounteous imagination. Every day can be re-created countless times. In the end, we don't know what's true. And yet it's all true, isn't it? It's a lifetime of possibility in one day."

Nico didn't know how to answer her. Now he wonders, will this book set him free? The experience itself matters so little after all these years. But the secret has become enormous, foul, rotting. Now he has swept up the mess of it and created poems. Could she really have called the poems lovely? Breathtaking? Nico wants to tell Chantal all of this.

"Is it like a mystery? A thriller?" Philippe asks.

"Who'd you get today?" Nico asks Philippe. Philippe lights up a cigarette.

"*Bof*," Philippe says. "No one. I've got my regular at eleven. No

one else. Clavère is trying to fuck with me. He wants me out
and he won't fire me. So he keeps telling me that he doesn't have
students for me. I am so fucking done with this school."
Philippe blows out a stream of smoke. His cheekbones hollow
and his face changes—for a moment, he looks haunted. Then he
smiles and again he looks handsome and self-possessed. Nico
imagines that he comes from money, despite his cheap shirt and
ripped jeans.

"You going to get another job?" Nico asks.

"I'm going to focus on my music. I've got better things to do
than babysit some American girl who can't conjugate the verb
être."

"The one with the tits," Chantal tells Nico.

"Ah-hah," Nico says. Philippe has told them that if it weren't
for the woman's breasts, he would not be able to stand his two-
hour sessions with her.

Nico looks at Philippe and Chantal across the small table and
notices something different: Chantal has edged her chair slightly
away from Philippe. She will not look at Philippe. Did she see
the kiss? he wonders.

Philippe and Chantal are lovers; Nico knows that. And yet he
can't quite believe it, now that he's spent some time with them.
They're shadow and sunlight. What would draw Chantal to the
dark corners of Philippe's life? But then he remembers the first
time he saw them together at a meeting at the school. They
stood against the wall in the back of the classroom. Philippe
wrapped his arms around Chantal and she leaned back into him.
They both looked dreamy and slow, as if they had spent the day
in bed together and had thrown on clothes at the last minute to
make it to the meeting. As their boss droned on about the chal-
lenges of teaching the Japanese, Philippe whispered in Chantal's

ear, and Chantal closed her eyes, snaked her arm around Philippe's back, and let her lips part as if ready to make a sound too intimate for such a public place. Nico remembers thinking: I want to know her.

Now they're both looking at him across the table, as if waiting for something.

"You got enough gigs to carry you?" Nico asks. He doesn't really know what Philippe does, music-wise.

"I auditioned a lead singer last night," Philippe says. "She rocked."

"And so you fucked her," Chantal says.

Nico has never heard Chantal curse. Finally, Chantal and Philippe glare at each other. Nico thinks: I shouldn't be here.

"I had a dream about you last night," Philippe says. "You were standing in the middle of the Champs-Élysées. Naked. A crowd of tourists were cheering and tossing coins at your feet."

"I slept with Nico last week," Chantal tells Philippe.

Nico looks at Philippe but says nothing. He hadn't imagined this. What had happened that night with Chantal was so personal, so private and contained, that he never thought about the possibility that she would tell Philippe.

"No problem, man. I don't blame you. She's hot. Look at her. You'd think that she's an uptight bitch. But she's really hot."

"Philippe," Chantal says. Her voice is mournful.

Nico remembers the surprise of Chantal's skin. He undressed her slowly that night while the boat rocked and the light of the summer moon filtered through the porthole. He had imagined a different terrain—white skin untouched by the sun, a long, thin body. But her skin was tanned and her body dipped and rose in lovely curves. She lay on her side and they faced each other. Though he waited for her to stop him, to change her mind and ask him to leave, she gave him permission with her watchful eyes, with her playful smile, with her silence. He ran his fingers along the rise and fall of her body, neck to shoulder to waist to hip to the long stretch of her glorious leg. The landscape of Chantal, he thought.

Revenge sex, he reminds himself. Chantal didn't need this morning's display on the street corner to confirm what she already knew.

"Tell us about your book, Nico," Chantal says.

He looks at her, surprised. She offers a strained smile. Has he lost her? Of course he lost her. He never had her.

"Not now," he says. "Tonight. I'll buy a bottle of champagne at La Forêt."

Nico remembers the euphoria he felt after the phone call yesterday from the editor. I'll tell Chantal, he had thought immediately. And through the long, restless night, he had imagined her pleasure at his news. He imagined her gentle questions, her admiration, her new respect. He had guarded his poems with a fierce secrecy and now, instead of enjoying the expansive pride he expected, he feels an odd sense of loss. Did he think he'd win her with poetry? Had he foolishly thought he had already won her with a night of sex?

"We'll meet at seven?" she asks. Of course. They always meet on Friday nights. But everything has changed.

The waiter arrives and places their coffee cups on the table.

"*Du sucre,*" Philippe says. The waiter always forgets to bring sugar.

"Will you come?" Chantal asks Philippe when the waiter leaves.

"Tonight? Who knows. By this evening you will have run off with your American," Philippe says.

"Enough," Chantal says, quietly dismissing him with a slight wave of her hand.

The waiter slides a bowl of sugar cubes onto the table as he hurries by. Philippe drops three into his cup. They all sip their coffee. Nico looks at the young couple at the next table; they are now kissing.

Finally Chantal looks up at Nico and says, "Champagne would be nice."

"Seven P.M., then."

"I'll be there," Philippe says, and he slams his empty espresso cup on the table.

Nico looks at Chantal. She gives him a smile that is filled with secrets. For him? He doesn't know her despite a night of lovemaking that has sent him into each day yearning for more. Does he yearn for more of her? He doesn't even know that. He is a fraud, a poet with no understanding of his own desires. Does he just long for desire? No, it's love he wants, he assures himself.

"I'm tired of Paris," Chantal says.

"Why?" he asks.

"There's too much noise. It's too gray. Sometimes I feel like I can't get enough air."

Nico looks around. Along the rue de Paradis he can see a *tabac*, a *papeterie,* and a *plombier* tucked in among the apartment buildings. It's a street like almost any street in Paris, and yet he loves the way the new sunlight hits the tall windows of the nineteenth-century buildings, the way the café spills into the street, the way the pedestrians rush past, all of them hurried and impatient. Paris has entranced him ever since he left Normandy at eighteen. He even likes the relentless rain. Today, though the skies are clear, he expects another onslaught of storms. The rain suits him—it keeps him inside on his days off, writing and listening to jazz. But of course Chantal would hate this weather. She is meant for sunshine.

"I'm going to London," Philippe says. "In September."

"You didn't tell me," Chantal says quietly.

"We've got a gig—I don't know, I might stay. We can record a demo tape there. My drummer has a friend who can get us into a studio."

"That's great," Nico tells him.

Philippe glares at him.

Nico reaches into his pocket for a couple of euros to pay for his coffee.

Chantal looks at her watch. While she reaches into her bag for money, she says, "I would move somewhere warm. Somewhere very green."

Philippe drops coins on the table and charges off, his messenger bag banging against his back. He doesn't say goodbye.

"Why did you tell him?" Nico asks Chantal.

"I'm sorry."

"I thought it was between the two of us."

"It never is."

"Why not?" He tries to see her eyes but she bows her head and swirls the last bit of espresso in her cup.

"We all bring so many people to bed with us. We're never alone."

"He's furious."

"Because I changed the rules. I'm not supposed to play the same game that he plays."

"And now? What game are you playing?"

Chantal looks up. She reaches out and touches his cheek. "I don't know. Philippe has made me into someone else. I would like to believe in love again."

They had talked for a long time in bed after making love that night. When Nico told her about his high school girlfriend, how they would sneak out of their houses in the middle of the night and sleep in the hayloft in the barn, Chantal had said to him, "Young love teaches you how to love. You're so lucky. Most of us spend years trying to learn the ways of love." Nico knows that Chantal believes in love. But she was drunk that night, she was cheating on her boyfriend, and she wants to forget what they did.

She stands up and gathers her things. With her purse over her shoulder, she starts off toward the métro station. She looks back.

"I am done with all this," she says. "I'm ready for whatever the day might bring." She offers a dazzling smile, something full of hope for something else, someone else.

Nico watches her leave. He tries to hold her in his view as long as he can. The sun ducks behind a cloud and then reappears, bathing the street in new light. Chantal disappears into the entrance of the métro. Nico pulls the paper out of his back pocket and opens it. *Josie Felton.* He looks at his watch. It is time.

Josie and Nico

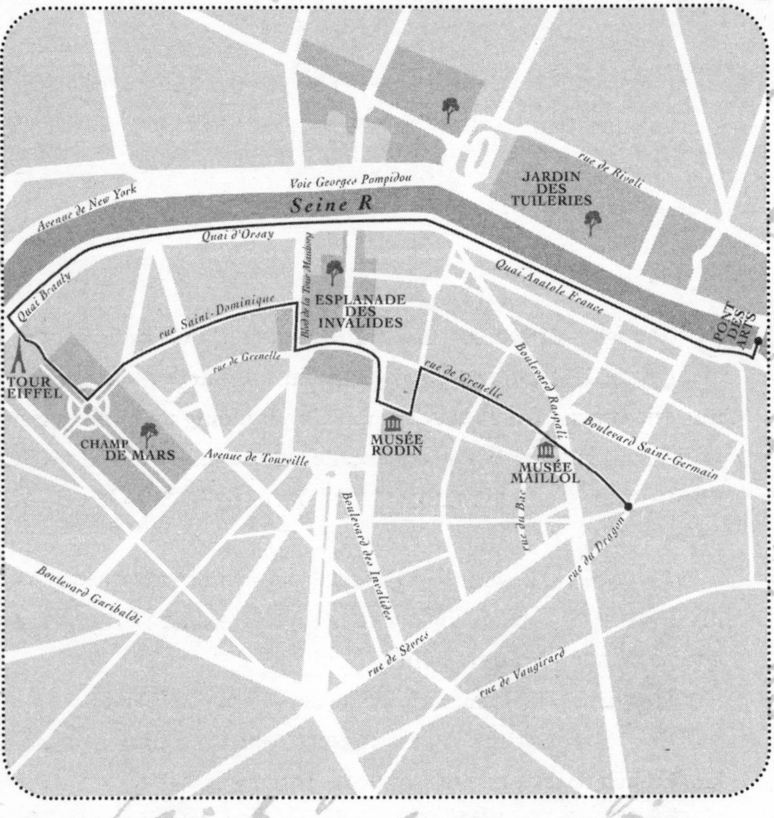
Voie Georges Pompidou
Seine R
rue de Rivoli
JARDIN DES TUILERIES
Avenue de New York
Quai d'Orsay
Quai Branly
Quai Anatole France
ESPLANADE DES INVALIDES
rue Saint-Dominique
rue de Grenelle
rue de Grenelle
PONT DES ARTS
TOUR EIFFEL
CHAMP DE MARS
Avenue de Tourville
MUSÉE RODIN
MUSÉE MAILLOL
Boulevard Raspail
Boulevard Saint-Germain
rue du Bac
rue du Dragon
Boulevard des Invalides
Boulevard Garibaldi
rue de Sèvres
rue de Vaugirard

*J*osie is surprised that her tutor is a man, that he is young, and that he is startlingly handsome. She considers walking back into the office of that horrible modern building and telling the waif behind the desk that she's made a mistake, that she doesn't want a tutor for the day, that she wants to go back to her hotel room and drink Orangina and vodka.

The tutor shakes her hand, and she's surprised by the heat of his skin—she has been cold for so many days. She pulls her hand away as if she's been scorched.

"So you're a French teacher," he says to her in French.

"*Oui*," she answers. "But it's been a long time since I've spoken French to anyone but American teenagers."

She doesn't say: It's been a long time since I've spoken at all.

She decided to hire a tutor only yesterday when she realized that after three days in Paris she hadn't said more than a few words—when ordering a croissant or a glass of wine or asking the hotel maid for an extra towel. Suddenly the prospect of a day of conversation terrifies her. She doesn't feel capable of conversation.

"Are you here in Paris for business or pleasure?"

It's a trick question. She has no business and she has no plea-sure. She quit her job three weeks ago. The man she loved died three weeks ago.

"I'm here to buy shoes," she finally answers.

He looks at her feet. She's wearing red Converse sneakers, the same shoes she always wears. Her students loved her shoes. Her old boyfriends, slackers one and all, loved her shoes. But Simon wanted her to buy grown-up shoes, pumps with three-inch heels, strappy sandals, red stilettos. And so he bought them tickets to fly to Paris.

"We'll go shopping," the tutor says.

"No, I was—"

"No reason to sit in a classroom," he tells her. "Paris is our classroom."

He looks around while she presses her hand to her stomach, which is contracting in fierce spasms. She doesn't want to get sick like she did yesterday on the métro. Yet another reason she should be back in her hotel room, under the musty covers.

"We'll take the bus," the tutor says. "More to see, more to talk about."

His enthusiasm is killing her.

"I'm Nicolas, by the way. Call me Nico."

"Josie," she says.

"Josie," he repeats, smiling, as if he's just discovered some-thing wonderful. "Let's buy shoes."

On the bus she loses herself in memory. Six months ago. She stood on the school stage, working with one of her students on the upcoming play. Josie looked up when the door to the theater opened and closed, letting in a flash of light and a glimpse of a tall man wearing a black suit. Silver hair. And then darkness again.

She looked back at the boy on the stage.

"Go ahead. Try it one more time," she said gently.

But the boy was peering into the darkness of the theater. Now he'd never speak his lines louder than a whisper. Take a shy boy and put him onstage—and what? He discovers his inner strength and transforms himself in front of his peers? What was she thinking in casting Brady as the lead? She was thinking of saving him, nothing less. But Brady, as cute and sweet and smart as he may be, cannot belt out his lines, cannot plant a loud smacking kiss on the lips of lovely Glynnis Gilmore.

"Dad," the boy said.

Josie looked into the darkness of the theater. The man was sitting there, somewhere. Damn him.

"Brady. Ignore your father. We have another fifteen minutes."

Brady looked at her, his eyes wide with fear. "I can't do it with him here."

Josie walked toward him on the stage. He stood against the papier-mâché stone wall as if it were holding him up. She would have to show him how to use the stage as if he owned it, not as if he were hiding among the props.

"He might be here opening night," she said quietly. "So will a lot of other people. You have to forget about that space. It's this space here that matters."

He nodded. His long straight hair fell in front of his face—his own private curtain. He was the kind of boy she would have loved in high school. Maybe that's why she chose him. Twenty-seven years old and she was still behaving like a teenager.

"Try the line again. To me."

He nodded. He held her eyes. He took in a gulp of air. He whispered, "I can't say the line to you. I can't say the line to anyone."

Love me. Love me. "Say it over and over again," she would tell him later. "Say it as if you're ordering her to do as she's told." But right then, with his father in the theater, she whispered, "Go on home. We'll work hard tomorrow."

"My son thinks you're wonderful," the man said. He looked at her with his green eyes and she looked at his mouth instead, then at the open V of his sweater. Gray sweater under a black suit. Silver hair that curled at the nape of his neck. She had nowhere to look.

"I think he's pretty great."

"You teach French and theater?" he asked.

"I teach French and I stumble around in the theater."

He smiled. He was handsome the way Brady might be some day. But this big, bold man could never have been shy or sweet. Was this the reason Brady couldn't claim his role onstage?

"Simon," he said, offering his hand.

"Josie." She shook his hand and felt his palm press into hers like a secret passing between them.

"Can he do this?" Simon asked, gesturing to the stage. Brady had gone to get his books and jacket. They were standing near the back of the theater. Josie had forgotten to turn on the lights. The dark room, the woody smell of the newly built set, the rows of empty chairs facing the other way—Josie already felt as if they were doing something illicit.

"Yes," Josie lied.

"Then you're really good," Simon said.

"Dad!" Brady called, bounding up the stairs.

"Nice to meet you," Josie said, turning to leave.

"Wait," Simon said.

She couldn't wait. She could barely catch her breath.

"Have a nice evening, you two." She slipped out the door.

Love me. She was sideswiped by it, she would later tell her friend Whitney. She leaned against the wall in the hallway, clutching the script to her chest. Some kid's dad. One sly smile and she was smitten.

"Don't even think about it," Whitney told her.

"It's all I can think about," she said on the phone that night. "I'll quit teaching and join the Peace Corps."

"You haven't done anything," Whitney reminded her.

"He'll call tonight," Josie told her.

"I have no good reason for calling you," he said.

"I have no good reason for talking to you," she told him.

They were both quiet for a moment. Josie had gone to bed an hour before, and had twisted her mind around him, his words, his eyes, the V of his exposed neck, until she lay there, exhausted, as if beaten by something. When the phone rang, her hand leapt at the receiver.

"And I don't do this," he said, his voice surprisingly unsure. "I don't call women—especially my son's teacher—at home late at night."

"You're married."

"I'm married."

"I'm joining the Peace Corps. I decided earlier tonight."

"Can I see you before you ship off?"

She could have said no. She could have said "I'll lose my job. I'll lose myself." But she said yes. Yes.

"How did you come to be a French teacher?" the tutor asks.

Nico. His name slips away, as easily as her concentration. He keeps talking, the bus rumbles along busy streets, passengers come and go, bumping past them, the smell of sausage fills the stale air, and every once in a while he stops talking and she is required to say something. *All of this used to be easy,* Josie reminds herself. *In fact, I used to do it so well.*

"My parents didn't have a lot of money," she tells the tutor in French. She and Nico speak only French and she is surprised by how natural that is, as if the foreign words are easier for her to find than English words now. "We never traveled. I read a book about a young girl in Paris and I wanted to be that girl. And so I started studying French as if I could change everything in my life by speaking a different language."

"Did it work?"

She looks at him. "No," she says. "But maybe I'll try again."

"Is this your first trip to Paris?"

"Yes," she lies. She had spent her junior year here, but she is tired of talking. There is nothing to say about that year unless she tells him about the boys, the sex, the hashish, the hangovers.

"Did you come alone?" he asks.

"No," she lies. "My friend Whitney is spending the day at art galleries." She has never been a liar before and now the lies spill from her lips. Whitney hates Paris, hates art galleries, and, in fact, hates Josie now. "If you sleep with him," Whitney had said the next morning, when Josie told her she was meeting Simon for a drink, "you're alone in this. He's married, he's old, and he's your student's father. I'm not getting on this love train with you, girl. I'm not even going to be there after the crash."

The crash.

"You will love Paris," the tutor says with his unending optimism. "I will make sure of that."

She looks at him, surprised.

"I hired a French tutor. Not an ambassador."

He doesn't stop smiling. "I don't charge extra for those services."

She looks away. She wishes he were less attractive, less eager. She would like to hate him, but here she is, following him off the bus as if this is exactly what she wants to do. They are in the heart of the bustling Sixth Arrondissement, at the carrefour de la Croix-Rouge, and she stops on the sidewalk, panic-stricken. What is she doing here? How can she take another step forward?

"Don't worry," he tells her. "The stores are too expensive here. We're just pretending."

Pretending? Did she misunderstand him? So far, everything she has done since Simon died has been a pretense. Everything except for the deep, bottomless sleep she stumbles into, as if plummeting off a cliff, every night.

"I don't understand," she says.

He takes her arm and moves her effortlessly across the street with the flow of people. She's astonished that it's so easy—he leads, she walks. Yesterday, without someone at her side, she stood paralyzed in front of the gates of Père Lachaise Cemetery for over an hour. She wanted to see—what? Jim Morrison's grave site? Oscar Wilde's tomb? Finally, she turned, threw up behind a tree, métroed back to her hotel, and burrowed back into her bed.

She shouldn't have come to Paris. She should have thrown away the plane tickets. The seat on the plane beside her was empty. Simon's seat, in business class, her constant reminder of what should have been. Champagne, wine, long conversations about Montmartre and Giverny, whispered promises, perhaps even a wandering hand under the blanket. Instead, she took two sleeping pills and awoke in Paris, groggy and disoriented.

"How about these?" the tutor asks. Nico. If she can remember his name, she can pull herself out of the slog of her mind and back to Paris. Shoes. He's holding a turquoise patent-leather shoe in front of her face. It's got a four-inch heel that looks like a dagger.

"Perfect," she tells him.

"She'll try these on," he tells a woman.

They're in a shoe store, but Josie can't remember walking in. The saleswoman knows that it's all a ruse. She's looking at Josie with contempt, as if her red Converse sneakers are sullying the white marble floor. Josie tells her she wears a size 38 and the saleswoman mutters "*Américaine*" under her breath.

Nico sits next to her on the zebra-striped bench.

"Your accent is perfect," he whispers. "It's the shoes that give you away."

"How much do the blue shoes cost?" she asks him.

"Your salary. Don't even think about it. We're playing a game."

"She knows."

"Who cares? There's no one else in this ridiculous store."

The store has plastic pigs hanging from the ceiling. Everything is patent leather, even the saleswoman's miniskirt and her go-go boots.

The woman places a box on the bench beside Josie. "We only have size thirty-nine." She walks away.

"Even my feet are too small for this place," she whispers to Nico.

"Your feet are perfect," he says.

"I have a boyfriend," she tells him. It slips out of her mouth.

"Of course you do," Nico says. He's unstoppable.

She's oddly pleased. For six months she could never say "I have a boyfriend." She couldn't say: "I'm having dinner with my boyfriend Wednesday night. My boyfriend is meeting me in San Francisco for the weekend. I'm going with my boyfriend to Paris." For six months her happiness was a secret. Now her grief is a secret. She had no right to the boyfriend. And she has no right to this grief.

Nico lifts the shoes from the box and hands one to her. It's an astonishing thing, this stiletto. She holds it in both hands, loving it.

"Put it on," Nico says.

She takes off her sneakers and slides one bare foot into the shoe. It fits; in fact, it hugs her foot and feels as sleek as a new skin. She needs a new skin. Maybe her new skin is a turquoise "fuck me" shoe. She puts on the other shoe and stands.

Her feet wobble. She giggles and the sound of her own laugh surprises her. She looks at Nico and feels herself blush.

"Look at you," he says.

She looks in the mirror. She's wearing jeans and a black tank top. The electric blue shoes transform her into someone else. She stands tall in the mirror, taller than she's ever been. She's lost weight in the past few weeks and she sees her own cheekbones, the clavicles below her neck. She's not a schoolteacher.

She's a woman with a boyfriend on a trip to Paris. He couldn't come but she'll bring back some shoes that he'll love. Josie smiles and the woman in the mirror smiles back. It's a devilish smile.

"I'll take them," she says.

Nico laughs. "I wish I could buy them for you."

"Seriously," Josie says. "I want them."

"They cost four hundred euros."

Josie's stomach somersaults; she thinks she might throw up. And in that second, instead of calculating the impossible cost of this pair of shoes, she counts weeks, weeks since she made love with Simon, weeks since her last period. She is pregnant. She knows this when she lifts her eyes in the mirror—from her wobbling feet to her belly. It's the same taut stomach, the same narrow waist. But now she's carrying Simon's baby.

"Let's go," she says to the French tutor. She can't remember his name. She teeters back to the bench on the perilous heels and drops down beside him. She can't get the shoes off fast enough. The saleswoman is smirking, leaning back against her perch by the desk, a pink-snouted pig hovering about her head.

Josie drops her head between her legs.

"Are you all right?" the tutor asks. He places his hand on her back. His hand is on fire and the heat spreads through her thin top, wraps around her body, and heats up her belly.

"No," she tells him, taking in deep, slow breaths.

"Hey, Josie. C'mere," Brady called from across the room.

She looked up. Brady usually called her Ms. Felton. She insisted that her students call her Josie and watched as they struggled with the name, a kid's name for a teacher, a young teacher who dressed like they did, a teacher who hated claiming authority for any reason other than that she earned it.

He was standing next to the snack table, holding a plastic glass as if it were a gin and tonic, his arm thrown around an attractive older woman. This was the new Brady, the star of the show.

Josie walked toward him, thinking, Yes, he'll be his father's son after all, there's the bold smile, the look-at-me tilt of the head. Josie stopped and someone bumped into her from behind. The attractive woman under Brady's arm was his mother. Josie was walking to meet her lover's wife.

"Mom, this is Josie. Ms. Felton. The director!"

Josie shook the woman's hand, looking at her hand, and then, seeing a diamond there, looked up, into warm eyes, a wide smile. A tiny half-moon scar on a high cheekbone.

"I want to thank you," the woman said. Her voice was deep and honeyed. A beautiful voice.

Josie, who always had something to say, was struck dumb. The woman's hand moved to her arm, holding her there.

"You did so much for him," she said in a conspiratorial whisper.

"Mom," Brady complained.

"He's good," Josie said, stupidly, as if that was all she could muster.

"He's amazing," the woman said. "But until today, no one else knew that. Just his father and I. Brady didn't even know it."

Josie stared at her.

"But you must have known," the woman insisted.

"Mom." Brady shook his head. "Parents and teachers should never meet. It's a mortifying experience."

"Have you met my husband?"

"No."

"Yeah," Brady said. "At rehearsal that day."

"I forgot. Did he come tonight?"

She knew he was in San Francisco. She would drive in and stay with him at his pied-à-terre tonight.

"He's got a meeting in the city," Brady said. "He'll come tomorrow night."

"You did a wonderful job," the woman said, her hand still holding Josie's arm. "At the point when Brady says, 'Do you love me'—or 'Will you love me'—what is it . . .'"

"'Love me,'" Brady says, his voice soft, his eyes hidden behind his curtain of hair.

"That's it," his mom went on. "When he said that to the girl—who was very good, what a beauty she is—well, I almost cried. I don't know why. It just . . . touched me somehow."

"It's a good moment in the play," Josie said.

The woman was lovely. She was warm and straightforward and vibrant. Josie had wanted a shrew. Instead, this woman smiled and said, "You have a gift."

They climbed the stairs to the third floor. Josie looked at every apartment door of this Russian Hill town house and silently pleaded, *Don't come out.* She couldn't imagine what Simon would say to his neighbors. This is my son's teacher! This is my lover! This is Josie. I just met her a couple of weeks ago and now I'm bringing her home for a quick fuck!

He unlocked the door to his apartment and she dashed into the dark room. He reached for the light switch on the wall and flicked it on, closing the door behind him. Then he wrapped his arms around her from behind.

"You're shaking," he said.

"I'm scared. I feel like a thief breaking into someone's house."

He turned her around. "Look at me." He lifted her chin.

She looked into his eyes and smiled. He made it easy. He looked so sure about this, as if there was no question in the world they should be standing here, wrapped in each other's arms, gazing at each other. Maybe her fears were childish, immature. An older woman would be able to do this without trembling knees.

"I met your wife," she said.

"Shh," he said, leaning down to kiss her. She could feel her heart pounding against his chest. And then, lost in the kiss, she forgot everything for a moment. When he pulled his mouth away, she caught her breath.

"What's wrong?" he asked.

"This is her place," Josie said.

"No. It's mine, really. I mean, it's ours, but she rarely uses it. I stay here when I have late meetings or early meetings. On a rare occasion we stay here when we come in for a show or dinner."

Josie pulled away from him and looked around. The room was masculine—all leather and dark wood, with a cool blue ocean painting that filled one wall. A model airplane hung from a wire in the middle of the room. Josie reached up and touched a wing; it spun in the air.

"I have a pilot's license," Simon explained. "That's a model of my Cessna."

Josie looked at him. "Your wife is perfect," she said. "I mean, she's not what I expected."

"What did you expect?"

"Someone I could hate."

"I didn't fall for you because I hate my wife."

"Why did you fall for me?" Josie turned away from the long, cresting wave of the painting and looked into Simon's eyes.

"I couldn't help myself," he said simply. "I saw you onstage that day—I don't know—I was starstruck. Can that happen?"

"Have you brought other women here?"

"No. I told you. I've never done this before."

"I'm an idiot. I believe you."

He pulled her into his arms. "I promise you."

They kissed and she pressed herself into his body, wrapping her arms low around his waist, pulling him closer. She felt too many layers of clothes between them. She started to pull off his coat.

"Wait. There's a Murphy bed. I have to pull it down."

She turned around, surprised. It was a one-room studio and, sure enough, there was no bed.

Simon walked to the wall unit, then slid the bookcases aside, revealing a bed built into the wall.

"Amazing," she said.

He pulled a cord and the bed descended gracefully. It was neatly made, with pale blue sheets and a gray blanket.

"I can't," Josie said. She could feel her throat tightening.

Simon looked at her.

"It's her bed. It's where you sleep with your wife."

"Josie."

She shook her head. "I feel like Goldilocks in someone else's house. I can't do this."

"The sheets are fresh. I made the bed this morning."

"No."

He came toward her and took her in his arms again.

"She'll never know," he said.

"Let's go. Somewhere else. Anywhere else."

Later, in their room on the fourteenth floor of the Clift Hotel, they lay in each other's arms after sex and Ghirardelli chocolate and scotch and more sex.

"How did Brady do?" Simon asked.

Josie looked at him. "I wondered why you hadn't asked."

"I should have been there."

"You'll come tomorrow."

"I didn't want to be there with my wife. I didn't want to stand next to her and shake your hand. She knows me too well."

Josie climbed on top of him. She looked down into Simon's face.

"We can't do this, can we?"

"We have to do this."

He pulled her face to his and kissed her.

"Why?" Josie asked.

"Because I have to trust this. I know what love is—I love my wife, I love my son—I won't lie to you. But I've never felt this— I don't know—*need. Desire.* I've never known this"—he pressed her close to him, finishing his sentence as a whisper in her ear— "before."

Josie watched him for a moment. "I don't know what this is," she said. "I've had boyfriends, but this is not what that was. What is this?"

"Kiss me," Simon said.

• • •

Josie can hear the shoe saleswoman and the tutor talking to each other. She hears the words *petite amie:* girlfriend. "Does your girlfriend do this often?"

The tutor doesn't correct her. "No," he says. "She's not feeling well today."

Josie rinses her hands in the tiny sink in the back of the store and considers slipping a pair of shoes into her bag. She has never shoplifted in her life, but who knows what she might be capable of now? The saleswoman didn't want her in the bathroom of her piggy store, but Josie had marched through the curtains anyway and found a toilet to throw up in rather than the white marble floor. She picks up a pair of red shoes—Dorothy-in-Oz shoes—and clicks the heels.

There's no place like home.

Why should she fly home on Sunday? Why not stay in Paris and become Nico's girlfriend and shoplifter of expensive shoes?

She puts the shoes back on the shelf. She steps back into the showroom.

"*Ça va?*" Nico asks. He looks concerned. Most of his students are not pregnant, crazy ladies, she assumes.

"*Ça va,*" she sighs, and offers a smile. Poor guy. He deserves better in a girlfriend.

"I don't want the shoes," she tells the saleswoman. "I seem to be allergic to them."

Nico nods and takes her arm, guiding her out of there.

"Does your boyfriend know?" he asks her when they are on the street, standing close to each other in the middle of a crowd of shoppers, all of them wearing extraordinary shoes.

She is not surprised; this tutor seems to be a jack-of-all-trades. Why shouldn't he also be able to guess her secrets? She shakes her head.

"Will he be happy?" he asks.

"Yes," she says, assuredly. "He will be very happy."

"Good," Nico says. "I once had a girlfriend who broke up with me and then, a month later, called to tell me she was pregnant. She wanted to have the baby. I told her I'd raise the baby with her. She said she was moving to Morocco and that she would send me pictures of the kid from time to time. I never heard from her again."

"That's awful."

"I think about it all the time. The kid would be three now. I wander through playgrounds looking for him. Or her."

Thunder rumbles through the skies.

"Let's find someplace to go," Nico says, "before it rains."

But the skies open immediately and the rain blasts them. Josie feels Nico's arm wrap around her back and move her along rue de Grenelle. She doesn't mind the rain; she doesn't mind his arm around her. She'll give herself up to this, she decides. It is easier than every day of the past weeks.

Nico opens a door and leads her inside. It is a small museum, though it looks nothing like a museum. It has vaulted ceilings and pale marble walls and floors. A sign reads: MUSÉE MAILLOL. A teenage boy chews gum behind a counter; he doesn't even look up. Josie glances around—she doesn't see anyone else in the building. Ahead of them is an enormous statue of a nude man.

Nico leads her to the desk and buys two tickets.

"I can pay," she says.

"No. Please."

The boy cracks his gum and pushes his comic book under the counter. He passes them the tickets and a brochure: *Marilyn Monroe: The Last Photographs.*

They walk past the turnstile. There is no one to take their tickets. When Josie looks back, the boy is reading his comic book again. For a moment, he looks like Brady, serious and shy. Brady before he became a star. Brady before.

She puts her hand on her belly. The nausea has passed, but now she feels light-headed, a little dizzy. She has never been pregnant, has never yet considered having a baby. She had thought that would be years away, when she was married and had moved from teaching to playwriting, her real passion. She had imagined a young husband, a cottage in the country, a couple of big dogs, and a vegetable garden.

But she's pregnant without the guy, the job, the house, the dogs. In fact, it's all she has. This baby.

She has no right to this baby. She thinks of Simon's wife at the funeral, her skin the color of ash, her eyes as flat as a lake. The woman didn't remember Josie. She nodded, accepting condolences that meant nothing. Nothing could penetrate that grief. What right did Josie have to her grief?

"She is tragic, no?" the French tutor asks.

Josie looks up. Marilyn Monroe stares back at her, her mouth slightly open, her eyes half closed. She looks drunk on sex, on booze, on death. She looks luscious and ripe and ready to die. Josie's eyes fill up. She steps back, away from the seductive stare. They're in a gallery space, full of Marilyn. Every photo—and the photos are huge, pressing the limits of each room—is of Marilyn. Marilyn with her head tilted back, a sated smile on her face. Marilyn drawing on a cigarette. Marilyn puckering up. Marilyn with her hand resting on the curve of her hip, stretched out on a couch, offering herself up. *Love me.*

"She killed herself three days after this photo shoot," Nico says, reading from the brochure.

"You can see that she was ready," Josie says.

"To die?"

"To give herself up to death. It looks like she was already dying."

"You will have the baby, yes?"

Josie looks at him. Nico. He has the kindest eyes. She imagines his sweet child with eyes like this. It's a boy and he's holding his mama's hand, walking through the market in Marrakesh. He's got a swoon of sand-colored hair and everyone stops to stare at the lovely child.

"Yes," she says. The minute she says it, she makes it true. "He's mine."

"It's a boy?"

"I think so," she says. She has Simon's boy in her belly. It's not fair. His wife has nothing. And she has this.

"Your boyfriend is very lucky."

She smiles. Her smile breaks and tears spill from her eyes.

"I'm sorry," Nico says.

"No, no. It's the photographs," Josie tells him. "They're so sad. Look at that one." She turns back to the wall and Marilyn's shadowed face. She can hear the rain against the glass roof that covers the courtyard. It sounds like an ominous movie score— there's an army approaching or a madman about to break into someone's house. She wraps her arms about herself. Her skin is still wet from the rain and she's suddenly chilled.

"Didn't she have an affair with your president Kennedy?" Nico asks.

"I think so," Josie says. "Apparently back in those days American presidents could get away with their indiscretions."

"Not anymore. Here we laugh at what happened to Clinton. Why should anyone care?"

"Except his wife," Josie says.

"Yes. It's a private problem. Not a public one. It has nothing to do with politics."

"I wonder," Josie says, staring into Marilyn's dreamy eyes, "what it has to do with. Why men cheat. Why they fall into bed with pretty girls."

"For the time that they're in the arms of a beautiful woman, they're invincible," Nico says.

"Then they should stay there," Josie says quietly.

"Are we still talking about your presidents?"

Josie doesn't answer. She wanders down the wall of Marilyn. She feels drunk on Marilyn, sexed up and sloppy, as if her own sheets have been thrown off the bed, exposing her.

Once, after making love with Simon at her cottage, she fell asleep. She woke up and saw him standing at the side of the bed, watching her. He was dressed, ready to leave, waiting to say goodbye. He couldn't wake her. He told her he stood there for a half hour, already late for a meeting, because he couldn't take his eyes off her.

"Come back to bed," she had said.

He did.

It's in Marilyn's mouth, it's in her eyes, it's in the curve of her generous hip. *Come back to bed.*

Nico's by her side.

"Do you have a girlfriend now?" she asks. *Une petite amie.* She loves the phrase in French. Little friend. Even a boyfriend is a *petit ami.* On her lips, the words taste as sweet as they sound.

"No," Nico says. "I was waiting for you."

"But I'm taken," she tells him. Their tone is as light as the smoke drifting from Marilyn's cigarette.

Here, in the room with Marilyn, everything reeks of sex. It's as if they've just done it and now, once again, are about to do it. *Come back to bed.*

"If you were taken," Nico says, "you wouldn't be so very sad."

"Why don't you have a boyfriend?" Josie's father had asked, showing up at her cottage the morning after she returned from San Francisco, the morning after her stay with Simon at the Clift.

He was sitting in her tiny kitchen, drinking coffee, probably his fifth or sixth cup of the day. He had driven up from San Jose to Marin to surprise her. It was the anniversary of her mother's death, but they would never speak of that. It would be there, the idea of it, in the air between them, all day. They would talk about her fancy job at the prep school, his lousy grocery store, her old best friend Emily who lives next to her old ma, his middle-of-the-night heart murmur, but they would never talk about her late mother, his wife.

"I don't have time, Dad. I'm working too hard."

"A young girl shouldn't work so hard."

"I like it," she told him, sitting across the table from him. "I *love* it."

"Love. Love is for boyfriends, not jobs."

He looked old, her father, his hair mostly gone, his skin mottled with age spots, his face jowly. She calculated: thirty-five years older than she was—and just ten years older than Simon. Impossible, she thought. Simon was fit and firm, though when he slept she saw that his skin relaxed in a way that surprised her. It seemed to let go of his bones and suddenly he was vulnerable, soft. Something about that moved her, as if he too needed someone to watch over him.

But her father was old and cranky and out of touch with her world. Simon didn't seem old to her. True, he was a world apart from the boys she usually fell for—the long-haired, rumpled, mumbling boys. The boys who come too quickly. The boys who throw on yesterday's clothes. The boys who live in basement apartments and smell of pot and beer.

"Are you taking care of yourself, Dad? You still go for walks every day?"

"You think I sit around and do nothing? You think I'm getting fat?"

"You're not getting fat, Dad. You look great."

"You're full of shit."

She smiled. This was what her parents did, this squabbling. He looked pleased as punch, as if he'd just flexed his muscles for an admiring crowd.

"I worry about you," he said.

"You shouldn't worry," she said gently. "I take care of myself."

"So who's the boyfriend?"

"There's no boyfriend, Dad. I told you."

"You got any cake? Coffee cake or something?"

Josie stood up and walked to the pantry. She took a loaf of whole wheat bread and sliced a couple of pieces, put them in the toaster. While she gathered jam, butter, plates, and knives, her dad told her about Emily's new boyfriend, a lawyer in San Jose.

"Good for Emily," Josie said, placing the toast in front of her dad.

"You and Emily used to be best friends. You couldn't go any-where without that girl."

"That was a long time ago, Dad."

"You call this coffee cake?"

"It's all I have."

"I should have told you I was coming. You could have bought me a cake."

"I would have bought you a cake, Dad," Josie said, smiling.

"I like a little surprise sometimes. But this is the price I pay." He held up the whole wheat toast.

"Put jam on," Josie urged him. "It needs a little something."

"So what happened with you and Emily?"

"Nothing, Dad. Life. We grew up. I moved away, she stayed home. People change."

"I don't change."

"Thank God for that."

"You making fun of me?"

"Never."

He smiled and she thought of her mother, sitting next to him, both of them short and a little fat, both of them fighting over every little thing, smacking each other's arms like some married version of the Three Stooges. Josie was always embar-rassed by them, embarrassed by her love for them, and then, when her mother died, she yearned for the noise of them.

"You could have a girlfriend," Josie said gently. "It's enough time."

"Ha," her father said. "You think there's another Franny out there somewhere?"

"No."

"One of a kind."

"I know. Maybe the next one is a different kind."

"There's no next one."

"You might try."

"You want Emily to ask her nice boyfriend if he has any friends at the law firm for you?"

"No, Dad."

The phone rang. She leapt at it.

"Hello."

"I miss you."

"My dad's visiting. Can I call you later?"

"No. I'm headed into the meeting. I just wanted to tell you—"

He didn't say anything. She waited. She watched her dad, who fiddled unhappily with his toast.

"Will he be there tonight?"

"No."

"I'll come by."

"No."

"Why?"

"Hey, Whitney. My dad wants me to start dating. You know any eligible single guys to fix me up with?"

"Don't."

"Okay. Give it some thought. He's right. I should have a boyfriend. I should fall in love with someone and bring him to meet my dad."

Her dad nodded, smiling, his lips smeared with boysenberry jam.

"I wanted to tell you I'm falling in love with you," Simon said.

"That's crazy," Josie said. "You must know some guys. The good ones can't all be married."

"Stop it."

...

"My father would like you," Josie tells Nico. They're standing side by side, gazing at a photo of Marilyn, naked, a sheer scarf draped over her body.

"Not your mother? It's usually the mothers I charm."

"My mother's dead."

She moves to the next photograph on the gallery wall—Marilyn taking a long, lazy drag on her cigarette.

"Lung cancer. Eight years ago. She never smoked a cigarette in her life."

"I'm sorry."

"My father smoked. Quit the day she was diagnosed. A bit late, though."

"You were so young."

"I'll tell you a story I've never told anyone. About my mother's death."

He looks pleased. This man is way too easy.

"That last winter my parents were in Palm Springs, staying with my aunt for a month. I flew down there a couple of days before my mom died and then flew back with my dad. They had my mother's body flown up—Dad wanted her buried at a cemetery near their house. I had packed my mother's clothes to have her buried in. When we were waiting for our luggage at SFO, standing in front of the . . ." Josie stops. She is suddenly there, waiting for the bags, no longer telling a story. It had been sweltering hot in Palm Springs and now it was frigid, even in the airport. Her coat was packed in her suitcase and she stood there, teeth chattering, waiting for the bags to arrive.

"Yes?"

"I don't know the word."

"What word?"

"For the thing that the suitcases drop onto. The— Oh my God, I can't even remember the word in English."

"Le carrousel de bagages?"

"Yes. 'Carousel.' That's the word."

"Tell me the story."

Josie feels panic stirring inside her. She looks around. Marilyn; a cigarette, a martini, puckered lips, long, manicured fingernails. Marilyn, Marilyn. She is drunk on Marilyn.

"We were all standing there, at the baggage claim, and first a shoe dropped down—not a suitcase, but a single shoe. It circled the carousel once and everyone watched it. When it passed by me a second time I recognized it. My mother's navy-blue shoe. Someone laughed. I grabbed it and tucked it under my arm, embarrassed somehow. And then a pair of underpants dropped from the chute—I'm not kidding—my mother's flowered underpants. The ones I chose from her drawer to have her buried in. Then her blouse. A peach-colored silk blouse she wore for special occasions. It almost floated down, as if worn by a fucking ghost. I grabbed each item and tucked the clothes in my arms. Her bra. Imagine: everyone was watching. Her C-cup rose-colored bra tumbled down. My father walked away. Finally my suitcase dropped down the chute and it was partially open, the items spilling out. I grabbed the bag and started stuffing everything back."

Josie's crying, tears running down her face, and she can't stop. Nico pulls her toward him and holds her. She lets him. She swipes tears from her face but there's no stopping them.

Simon's gone.

...

"I've been sitting in my car across the street. I waited until your father was gone."

Josie reaches out and places her hand on Simon's chest.

"I wanted to walk up to him and say, 'I'm Josie's boyfriend. She doesn't need another boyfriend.'"

"But it's not true. You're not my boyfriend. You're someone's husband. You're the man I sneak away to have sex with. You're the reason I can't even talk to my best friend anymore."

"Don't."

"I can't give my father the one pleasure he wants."

"I know, Josie. That's why I sat in my car for the past two hours."

"You have Brady's play tonight. It starts in an hour."

"I can't go."

"This can wait. Brady can't wait."

"I can't give you more than this."

"I know that. I'm not asking for more."

"You're asking for a man to introduce to your father."

"Why are you here? What do you want?"

"I want you."

"It stopped raining," Nico says. "Let's go have lunch."

Josie finds a Kleenex in her purse and wipes her face. She has stopped crying but she feels raw. When she first learned about Simon, when Whitney called that Saturday morning and told her to turn on the television, she couldn't cry—or scream or rage. She sat stunned, in front of her computer, Googling news reports, trying to find out everything she could about the crash of a small plane in the mountains near Santa Barbara. The phone kept ringing and she never answered it. Later there were dozens of messages from other teachers, a couple of Brady's classmates, even a long, sobbing message from Glynnis Gilmore. She had fallen in love with Brady on opening night, she said.

Now a ridiculous memory of her mother's death has un-moored her. And the French tutor has galloped in on his white horse.

They leave the museum in a hurry, as if chased by Marilyn's hungry eyes. The boy at the front desk doesn't even look at them as they leave.

"I know a restaurant," Nico says, and he takes her arm, moving her quickly along the slick city streets. The sun reflects off puddles and wet cars; Josie digs into her purse for her sunglasses. She's disoriented, her mind swimming in too many dark holes: her mother, Simon, Marilyn. She needs to come up for air; her lungs are bursting with the effort.

"*Voilà,*" Nico pronounces, as if he created this restaurant on this corner, as if he's responsible for its charming yellow walls, the pale blue tablecloths, the profusion of flowers. He's transported them to Provence and Josie takes a deep breath.

"You like it?" he asks proudly.

"Very much."

"I knew you would," he says.

They're seated in the back corner of the small room, and Nico orders a *pichet* of rosé wine.

While he speaks to the waitress, Josie follows the dark path of memory to his funeral. Even this cheery restaurant can't save her.

She remembers Simon's wife—Brady's mother—standing in the front of the church. The woman stepped away from her sisters and mother and friends and stood in front of the two coffins. No one dared to join her side. This was her grief, her devastating loss. She fell to her knees and wailed, a sound that echoed in the church. Josie turned and walked back to her car, parked almost a mile away since the crowd was so enormous. In that long walk she clenched her hands until her nails dug into the skin of her palms and bled. She had lost Simon and now she had lost the right to her grief.

Love me. Josie had never known that she needed the kind of passion in life that tipped her off balance, that carried her aloft. She had always thought of herself as a little too flimsy for love. With Simon, she lost her bearings, she gave herself up to love. And it filled her, made her weightier, fuller, richer.

"My boyfriend died," she says aloud.

Nico looks at her, surprised. The waitress arrives with the *pichet* of wine and they are silent while she fills their glasses. She places menus on the table and walks away.

"I lied," Josie says. "I'm not here with a friend. I'm alone. I was supposed to come to Paris with him. Simon."

"What happened?" Nico asks gently.

"Three weeks ago he took his son, Brady, down to Santa Barbara to look at the university. Simon flies his own plane—he's good, he's been flying for years. They don't know what happened. The plane went down in the hills above Santa Barbara. Both of them were killed."

"My God."

"I haven't been able to talk about it with anyone. First he was my secret. Now my grief is my secret. I was his lover, not his wife."

"It's his baby."

"Yes. I didn't know. But I'm sure I'm pregnant."

Nico reaches a hand across the table and places it on Josie's hand. Her face is streaked with tears again.

"He has a lovely wife. She lost everything. I lost a lover. I don't have a right to this grief. He wasn't mine. Brady wasn't mine. I was stealing someone else's love."

"I don't think you were stealing love."

"His wife deserved his love. His wife deserves this grief. I'm nobody. I went to the funeral because I was Brady's teacher. But that's a ruse, that's a lie. No one knows about me. And if they did, they'd hate me."

"It doesn't matter what anyone else knows. Or what they think."

"You're a stranger. You're French. What do you know?"

Nico laughs and suddenly Josie laughs, surprising herself. She drinks her wine, which is as light and cool as a breeze.

"Let's go to Provence," she says.

"For a French lesson?" Nico asks, smiling.

"Yes," Josie says. "Run away with me."

"Avec plaisir," Nico says, and the waitress stands before them, her pen poised above her pad.

Nico orders for the two of them, though he glances at Josie to make sure she agrees. She nods her approval.

"Today?" Nico asks when the waitress leaves. "On the next train?"

"Why not?"

They clink glasses.

"Maybe I shouldn't drink," Josie says. "The baby."

"In France they say a glass or two of wine is good for the baby."

"Bien sûr," Josie says, and she drinks.

She feels giddy, as if the wine has already made her light-headed. Maybe it's the words that echo in her head: *My boyfriend died.* She finally has spoken the words.

"There is no friend at the art galleries today?"

"Whitney doesn't approve of affairs and she can't stand contemporary art. She's at home in San Francisco, thinking I got
what I deserved."

"Leave her there," Nico says. "I'm glad we won't have to
bring her to Provence with us."

"And there is no one expecting you home for dinner
tonight?" Josie asks. They are flirting—it's a game, a life raft, a
way out of the mess she's in. She is talking again, she's crying,
she's even laughing. What could be wrong with this? She sips
her wine and leans close.

"Sometimes I meet two other tutors for drinks in the Marais.
We complain about our students and drink too much. Sometimes we go home and have sex with each other."

"All three of you?" Josie's eyes open wide.

"No," Nico says. "I'm not very interested in the other man.
It's his girlfriend I love."

"My God," Josie says. "We're a mess. All of us. Why is love so
complicated?"

"Today isn't complicated," Nico says, raising his glass. "This
is the first day I have enjoyed myself in a very long time."

They clink glasses again. The waitress arrives and places
bowls of mussels in front of them. She tucks tall glasses packed
with *frites* between the bowls. The table is suddenly filled with
wonderful-smelling food.

"I haven't eaten in a very long time," Josie says.

The first time Josie met Simon, alone, the day after Brady's rehearsal, they sat for a short time at a restaurant in a town far from
where they both lived. They ordered drinks—martini for Simon,

white wine for Josie—and then ordered dinner: steak for Simon, grilled salmon for Josie. The food sat there, untouched, while they leaned toward each other and talked. Simon asked questions—Who are you? Where do you come from? Why do you teach?—as if he were feasting on her rather than mere food. And Josie talked, as if she had never talked before, never told her story. When she said her mother died, he didn't skip on to the next subject the way her boyfriends had. He asked her about her mother's final week, about her father's sadness, about the gold wishbone she wore around her neck that had belonged to her mother. The waiter asked them if there was anything wrong with their dinners.

"No, no," they both said. "We're fine. Everything's wonderful."

And still, they barely touched their food.

"What do you do on a perfect day?" Simon asked.

"I hike into the hills," she told him. "I pack a picnic lunch and book and find a place to read by the river."

"Take me," he said.

He told her about flying, about the remarkable feeling of space and lightness and speed. He told her how he felt both reckless and safe at the same time—as if he could go anywhere, do anything, and yet he was master of his universe, completely in control.

"Take me," she said.

But the only place they ever went was to bed—her bed, hotel beds, motel beds, a futon bed he carried to the middle of a field in the hills of West Marin. That first night they left the food on the table and too much money thrown onto the check and they drove for a long time. They found a country cabin, one of a small group of log cabins for rent on the side of a lake. Josie stayed in the car while Simon went into the office, but she could see the woman peering at her through the window. Josie looked away, fiddled with the radio, worried that her body would never stop trembling from so much desire.

When Simon returned to the car with a key in hand he said, "She asked if I was traveling with my daughter."

"What did you say?"

"I said no. I don't want to get arrested for what I'm going to do to you tonight."

"She'll never know."

"She'll know. The whole world will know."

Josie was never loud in bed. She once bit the neck of a boyfriend in college. Better that than scream. She liked sex—it was a kind of game, a kind of athleticism that she was good at. But she didn't know what it was to give herself to someone, to abandon herself, to take someone in.

That night she made enough noise for the woman to ask Simon in the morning: "Was everything all right in there?"

"Fine," Simon said. "Everything was perfect."

"How did you know?" she asked Simon weeks later. "That first time. How did you know what would happen when we made love that night?"

"I couldn't stop trembling," he said. "All through dinner. While we drove to the cabin. My body was electrified. I had never felt anything like it."

"That never happened to you before?" Josie asked.

"You never happened to me before."

Josie and Nico feast on mussels and fries. They lick their fingers, they toss shells into the bowl, they sop sauce with the hearty

crusts of bread. When they are done the waitress brings a tangy
green salad and a cheese plate, and more bread, this time filled
with walnuts and cranberries.

Nico tells Josie about his childhood in Normandy, on a small
farm, how once he got drunk on Calvados and fell asleep in the
root cellar until morning. When he woke up he saw the police
were everywhere, combing the grounds of the house, talking to
neighbors, leading dogs into the woods.

He hid for a day, and at night he sneaked out and back into
the woods. He wandered home minutes later and his parents
rushed to embrace him.

"Where were you? What happened? Did someone take
you?" they asked.

"I don't know," he said.

They determined that he had blocked out some terrible
memory and for years after that, his parents, his friends, the
neighbors, all treated him as if he carried some dark secret
within him. His secret was his shame, that he had fallen asleep
in a dark corner and that he had caused so much commotion
over nothing.

"Did you ever tell them?" Josie asks. "Wouldn't they now
rather know that nothing bad happened to you?"

Nico shakes his head. "I've written a series of poems about
that night," he says. "Eventually they'll read the poems. But
even then, there's no true story. I can't undo the lie."

They eat three kinds of cheeses—a runny, pungent Camembert, an aged chèvre that tastes like the earth, and a Roquefort
that reminds Josie of her father, a man who eats bland food and
sprinkles his salad with blue cheese.

"Our parents don't know us," Josie says. "They can't know
us. We hide ourselves from them. Once they knew everything

about us and in order to escape them we keep our secrets, our private selves."

"Did you escape your parents?" Nico asks.

"I had to. I was desperate to. They wanted me to go to San Jose State College and live at home. But I wanted to be a continent away from them. I thought they were old-fashioned and uneducated and—*quelle horreur!* I wanted to be a French girl! I wanted to be a sophisticate! I went to NYU and a year later my mother got sick. I should have stayed closer to home. I should have taken care of her that year. My father needed me."

"You couldn't have saved her."

"No, but I could have saved my father."

"I doubt it, Josie. You might have helped the burden, but you wouldn't have made a bit of difference when it came to what he lost."

Josie looks at him, surprised.

"How do you know?"

"I'm listening to you. I'm imagining your life."

"But it's more than that. How do you know about grief?"

"I don't know," Nico says. "My parents are alive. I've never lost someone I loved. I just think I know about you."

"Is that because we're strangers? I can tell you about Simon and you can tell me about your night in the cellar. We'll disappear. It doesn't mean anything. It's like talking to a stranger on a plane."

"No. I'm right here. I'm listening to everything you're saying."

Josie looks around the restaurant. For a long time, the noise of other people's conversations had faded, along with the clang of silverware, the soft music of a violin concerto. She had lost the world and found Nico—not a lover, not even a boyfriend for a night or two, but someone to talk to.

"Thank you," she says.

"Don't think I do this for all my students," he tells her, smiling.

"You haven't even corrected my French."

"Your French is perfect."

"Now you're lying. Let's not tell any lies today."

"Then you should make your vowels more precise. They tend to float between consonants."

"Really?"

"I wouldn't lie."

"All these years I've been speaking French with floating vowels?"

"You had no one to show you the way."

Josie looks down, suddenly shy. He is smitten and she will leave him. She's just promised that she won't lie. And yet there is a lie in everything they share today. Because she won't go to Provence with him. It's another Josie who could catch the next train and curl up in a *couchette* with this blue-eyed Frenchman. This Josie—the one who lost Simon and quit her job, lied to her father, flew to France by herself—this Josie isn't capable of anything more than a day with a French tutor.

But she has finally eaten a meal and had a conversation.

"I won't ask for my money back from the school," she tells Nico. "You've taught me something after all."

"We're not done," he tells her.

Simon called her at school though she had told him not to. She could no longer focus on her work. She whispered into her cell phone, "I can't talk. I have class in two minutes."

"Meet me at the lake," he whispered back. "At four."

"I can't," she told him. "I have advisory."

"Cancel it," he said, and he hung up, so sure he was in the knowledge that she'd risk her job to see him. She canceled her meeting. She had canceled so many meetings, she had cut out of soccer practice even though she was supposed to be the assistant coach, and she had told the senior drama class that they should prepare their one-act plays on their own and that she'd step in to supervise in the final week. After three years as star teacher she was suddenly the slacker, the fuckup. She kept telling herself that she'd make up for it—this affair can't go on forever—and besides, she needed Simon more than she needed this job. There are other jobs.

She met him at the lake where they first started their affair, an hour's drive from the school. They'd been back a few times and Simon always asked for the same cabin. It was unseasonably cold and no one was renting these shacks, so the nasty woman who ran the place should have been happy to get their money. Instead, though, she asked Simon the same question every time. "Is that your daughter?"

Josie had never stepped into the office, had never seen the woman face-to-face, but she always felt the woman's eyes on her back as they rushed into the cabin moments later.

"One of these days I'll take you for a grown-up haircut," Simon said. "I'll buy you high-heeled shoes and we'll toss those silly red things in the lake. I'll buy you a cashmere sweater and wool slacks."

"And then you'd lose interest in me," Josie said. "I'd look like all the women you know. Your wife and your wife's friends. Your business associates."

"My wife—"

"I'm sorry," Josie said. The unspoken rule. The unspoken wife. Off limits. Keep her out of the bedroom, the cabin, the motel room, off the futon in the middle of the field.

"Come here," Simon said, and she stepped into his arms, silencing both of them.

Josie began to pull him toward the bed, but he resisted, smiling mischievously at her.

"We're not going to bed," he said. "Yet."

"I can't wait," she told him. "I've already buried my face in your neck."

She loved the smell of him, the soapy, musky Simon smell of him, and had told him that she could live off it, that if she could breathe him in every day she'd never need food again. "You're losing weight," he had told her. "Then let me breathe in more of you," she had said.

"You have to wait. I rented a rowboat."

"It's freezing!"

"I have blankets. I brought a thermos of hot buttered rum."

"You've done this before."

"Stop."

It was the other taboo, the other locked door. She didn't believe that she was his first lover. He was too good at it. He knew how to have an affair and she was a novice, a child in an adult's world.

"I've never loved like this," he would insist.

"How have you loved?" she'd ask him. "Tell me."

"No. Stop. Believe me."

She never believed him.

Now he took her hand and led her out of the cabin. He retrieved a duffel bag from the trunk of his car and threw it over one shoulder. They walked toward the lake, which was shrouded in fog, a cold, damp fog that chilled her despite the down jacket she wore. The sky was bleached gray and the lake was the color of iron. A rowboat bobbed on the water at the end of the dock, candy-apple red, astonishing against all that muted color.

"The oars are in the boat!" a voice called, and they both turned toward the office. The old lady stood there, arms locked across her heavy chest, squinting at them.

"Thanks!" Simon called back.

The woman kept her eyes on Josie. The look was hateful, as if Josie had stolen all the good men from all the older women in the world.

"She scares me," Josie whispered to Simon.

"Ignore her," he said.

"I can't. I can feel her watching me."

But the door slammed behind them and the old crone was gone.

Simon held the side of the boat and Josie climbed in. He placed the duffel bag on the floor of the boat. Then he stepped in and took the oars.

"Grab some blankets," he told her. "Stay warm while I row."

She pulled out a Hudson Bay blanket, a couple of fur hats, and the thermos. She placed a hat on Simon's head and leaned over to kiss him.

"Put yours on," he said.

She pulled the hat low on her head and was immediately warmer. She took a swig from the thermos and the sweet, thick liquid spread through her body.

She passed it to Simon, who paused mid-row, drank, smiled, and then rowed again. After a few moments, the world around them vanished and they were engulfed by fog. The colors around them bled into one another—sky, fog, water—and only the red outline of the boat held them in, containing them.

Simon stopped rowing. At first the boat moved, rocking slightly, and then it slowed and finally stopped. They were silent and the only sound they could hear was the call of a crow somewhere far away.

"I want to make love to you here," Simon said, his voice soft in the hushed air.

"It's so cold."

"We'll bury ourselves in blankets."

"We'll tip over and drown and no one will ever find us."

"Then we better not thrash around."

"Impossible."

"We'll do our best."

They drank more hot rum and they cocooned themselves in blankets on the bottom of the rowboat. They shimmied out of their clothes and the boat rocked. Icy water splashed against the side of the boat. They giggled and passed the thermos back and forth and held each other under the blankets, their bodies naked and electric. Josie was both cold and warm, scared and thrilled, energized and terrified of moving. When Simon ran his hand along her thigh, her hip, her stomach, she felt more than she had ever felt before—as if her nerve endings were jagged, exposed. His breath on her neck, his mouth on her breast, his hand between her legs, and the need to keep still, to restrain herself, as if any movement would plunge her into the black lake, made her feel as though she were caught in the whirling white fog around her.

When he slid inside her they kept very still and she could feel his deep breath; she could see his face looking down at her, his eyes holding hers.

"Don't move," he said, smiling.

When she came she felt her body exploding within, as if containing herself created something deeper, bigger, more seismic. And then he came, and kept coming, and the boat rocked and the water held them and the fog held them and the heavy sky held them.

He eased himself down and she felt his weight and the heat of his body.

Suddenly there was a cacophony of sound as if the birds had discovered them there, in the middle of their lake. The caws and screeches and trills were deafening, and though they turned their heads skyward, they couldn't see a thing.

"It's us making all that noise," Simon said. "Echoes from orgasms."

"That's just what it sounds like inside me," Josie said.

"I know," Simon told her. "I just didn't know everyone else could hear."

It was later, back in the cabin, when they had taken a long, hot bath and finished the thermos of hot rum, that Simon said, "I love you," and Josie said, "Don't leave me."

Nico looks up at the sky. Clouds linger, and somewhere in the far distance they can hear the grumble of thunder.

"We're safe," he says. "For a short while. Shall we try to walk to the train station?"

"We could walk to Provence," Josie says.

"I've never been a patient man," Nico says. "Put me on the fast train."

"Then let's walk to the train station."

She doesn't know if he is serious. She doesn't know him. She doesn't know herself these days, nor does she understand much of the ways of the world. So why not walk to the train station?

"What about my shoes?" she asks. Her red high-tops are wet from the rain and her feet are damp and cold.

"We'll buy them in Provence. We have many things to accomplish today. Make your vowels more precise. Run away together."

"I don't even know if you speak English," Josie says.

"Does it matter?"

"Not at all. In fact, don't tell me. We need one secret between us."

"Do you have a secret?"

"I've told you all my secrets," she says.

"Tell me about the book you read when you were young. The book that made you want to come to Paris."

"Can we sit down? My stomach—"

"Are you going to be sick?"

"I don't know. We started out too quickly. I'm not used to eating."

Nico leads her across the street and into a building. She's confused. Is he looking for a bathroom? It's a museum—Rodin—but she doesn't want to walk through a museum right now. He buys two tickets for the gardens, one euro each, and leads her outside again, into a lovely open space. There's a long expanse of lush, verdant lawn and a wide basin at the far end. She's stunned. Right here in the middle of Paris they've been transported to Eden.

Nico walks with her slowly across the long lawn and they find two lounge chairs at the water's edge. Josie sits and sighs; her stomach roils.

"Shall I get you some water?"

Josie glances off to the right—there's a café in the garden.

"No. Sit with me a moment."

He sits beside her.

"Perhaps the baby doesn't love wine after all."

"Impossible," Nico says.

She glances at him; he looks worried.

"I'm fine," she assures him. "I'm a little tired. My body isn't used to food."

"Take your time. This is a good place to rest."

They look out into the park. A crowd gathers around a sculpture, and Josie sees the head of *Le Penseur* towering above the mere mortals below. Other sculptures dot the landscape but Josie doesn't care about them. She loves the green water in the basin, the long stretch of green lawn, the abundance of green leaves on the rows of trees. A gust of wind stirs the air around her and with it the smell of newly cut grass. She's wrapped in her green blanket.

"I read the book so many times I could still probably recite the first paragraphs," Josie says. "But I'll spare you. It's an odd little story. A young girl loses her parents in the Champ de Mars. She looks everywhere for them—and then she decides that they've gone up to the top of the Eiffel Tower without her. But she's scared of heights. She can't go after them. So she waits and waits. Finally it begins to get dark and her parents never appear. With terror in her heart, she begins to walk up the stairs of the tower."

"Why doesn't she take the elevator?"

"There are only steps. This is fiction."

"Of course."

"She walks and walks, and the higher she climbs the more frightened she becomes. But she can't go back. She has to decide which is more frightening—life without her parents or climbing to the top of the tower. She keeps climbing. The sky darkens and night falls and soon all the lights of the city come on and there are as many stars below her as there are above. She's never seen anything so beautiful in her whole life. She forgets that she's scared and she runs to the top of the tower. There she circles the observation deck, looking up to the sky and down to the city streets with all the brilliant lights. She has no fear—she's on top of the world."

Josie pauses and takes a deep breath. Her stomach tightens and releases.

"Are you okay?"

"I'm fine."

"And the girl on the top of the Eiffel Tower?"

"A guard comes up to her. 'Mademoiselle,' he says. I loved that word when I was little. It was my first French word. Mademoiselle. 'Oui, monsieur,' she says. She's a very well-mannered little girl."

"Is she American?"

"Oh, no. She's very French. She lives on the edge of the Champ de Mars and she's never ever gone up to the top of the Eiffel Tower. Now here she is. And she can see all of her city below her."

"Her parents?"

"You *are* impatient," Josie scolds. "So the guard tells her that the tower is closing and she'll have to climb down again. She tells him that she's lost her parents. He promises her that they'll be waiting for her at the bottom of the tower. So she climbs down the many, many stairs, as happy as can be, because she's no longer afraid of anything. At the bottom of the tower she steps out and it's Paris and everything she's ever known, but it all

looks magically different now. She doesn't see her parents anywhere and she skips home, imagining a life without parents.
Maybe she'll never go to school! Maybe she'll kiss the boy she
likes! Maybe she'll wear the purple tights her mother hates!
When she gets to her house she looks up into the window of
her living room and she sees her parents standing there, under
the bright chandelier, looking out. They don't see her. She looks
back at the Eiffel Tower. It's sparkling with light. It's positively
luminous. When she looks back at her own house the lights go
out."

Josie smiles and rests her hands on her belly.

"That's the end?" Nico asks.

"The end. In big, swirly letters. *La fin*."

"This is a French book?"

"Of course it is. If it were an American book the girl would
never be allowed to climb the stairs alone and the guard would
have taken her to the police station, and even if she ran away
and got home and saw her parents in the window she would
have run to them and promised to never ever get lost again."

"You think that's it? She doesn't go home again?"

"It's not clear. Maybe she does. Maybe she doesn't."

"I think that's a terrifying story," Nico says.

"There you go. *Vive la différence*."

"Between boys and girls?"

"Between a nice young Frenchman with blue eyes and a
crazed American woman."

Nico reaches over and tucks a strand of hair behind her ear.

"You're not crazy."

"And that's another thing. I need a haircut," Josie says.

"Perhaps we can do that." His fingers linger briefly in her
hair.

"All in one day?" Josie asks.

"And you thought I was a mere French tutor."

Josie sees Nico's mischievous glance and notices how young he looks. There are no creases in the corners of his eyes. She has spent so many months looking into Simon's eyes.

"I made up that story," Josie tells him. "There is no book. There never was."

Nico smiles. "Perhaps you're not crazy, but you're very creative."

"I think the little girl never goes home. I think she finds the guard and asks him to take her home with him."

"That might be dangerous."

"But he's a very nice man. He owns three dogs, all of them bigger than the little girl. They live together in his tiny apartment on the top of a hill in Montmartre."

"What about her parents?"

"You're so responsible," Josie complains.

"I would miss my little girl," Nico says.

"Of course you would." She remembers that Nico has a child somewhere in Morocco, a child he's never seen. She thinks of Nico as a child, lost in the root cellar, his parents searching for him. This is a man looking to be found, she thinks.

Simon stroked her back. They were sprawled in bed, post-sex, pre-sex, all of their time together a blur of sex. They were in San Francisco, at yet a different hotel. Simon saw someone he knew at the Clift and Josie had to pretend she was a stranger, asking directions to a club. "Sorry," he told her, the friend in earshot. "I can't tell you anything about clubs in this city. I'm an old man. Why don't you ask the concierge?" Later Simon told her that the friend had said, "That girl is hot," and Simon had said, "I hadn't noticed."

"Of course you wouldn't," the man had said. "You're the last married man in America."

Simon had informed his wife about a series of Saturday meetings—he'd invented a nonprofit group that needed his expert help. He'd told his admin not to schedule anything for him at the end of the day on Friday because he needed to get back to San Rafael for a project he was working on with Brady. He was lying to everyone, and he did it with such ease that Josie thought he must be lying to her as well.

"How do you know this is love," she asked, "rather than love of sex?"

He ran his tongue up the line of her spine.

She rolled over and faced him. "You said you loved me."

"I do."

"Maybe you just love sex with me."

"I do."

"Why is it that now that I have love, I'm immediately scared of losing love?"

"You think too much. Stop thinking."

"When we make love I stop thinking."

"Then let's make love. It's been too long."

"Does this—does sex—matter more than anything else? Does it matter more than raising kids and having dinner parties and going to Cabo on vacation?"

"I wish I could do all of that with you."

"But you can't."

"You wouldn't even want it, Josie. You're twenty-seven years old."

"I don't know."

"Please. Come here."

"I'm right here."

"Come closer."

"Did you have this with your wife?"

"Don't."

"I've never had this before."

"I know, Josie. I've never had it before either."

"But you trust it? You can tuck it inside of you and take it home with you?"

"We have to. There's no other way."

"Let's make love really slowly. Let's make love so it lasts for hours and hours."

"It does," Simon said. "It lasts for days. It lasts for all the time that I'm not with you."

Josie moved into his arms.

"A haircut," Josie says, pushing herself up off the lounge chair. "Off with her hair!"

"You feel better?" Nico asks, eyeing her warily.

"I do." She puts her hands on her back and stretches, arching her back. She can feel the sun on her face. "Where shall we go?"

Nico stands and leads them to the exit of the Rodin Museum.

"There are lots of shops on rue Saint-Dominique. We'll find something there."

"Do you mind?"

"Of course not."

"Does your language school have rules about this sort of thing?"

"What do you mean?"

"How to spend your day with a client. Is my wish your command?"

"It's not usually so complicated. Most students are happy to learn the names of vegetables at the market."

"Have you ever fallen in love with a student?"

Nico smiles. "Before today?"

"You're not in love. You're a wonderful flirt, though. You can put that on your résumé."

"Isn't it possible that it's love?"

"What about your French tutor? Aren't you in love with her?"

"She has Philippe. I was just a diversion."

"But you love her. You could love her."

"I could love you."

"No. It's just a foolish question. I drank too much wine. Let's find a hair stylist. I can't go to Provence looking like a teenager."

Josie's hair is long and straight. She carries a clip in her purse, and when she's warm she twists her hair and pins it to the top of her head. When she lets it down it falls to the middle of her back, a horse's mane of deep chestnut that swings as she walks. She has never cut her hair more than a few inches.

They walk across the esplanade des Invalides and Nico reaches up and runs his fingers through her hair. She looks at him, surprised. It's as intimate a touch as she's felt in weeks. It stirs her and then angers her. She doesn't want to remember.

"It's a nuisance," she says, tossing her head and stepping away from his hand. "I'm done with all that."

"A shame," Nico says.

"*Voilà,*" Josie calls after they've turned onto rue Saint-

Dominique. She points across the street. "Perfect." It's a small salon, with a sign in the window that promises a *shampooing et coupe* for twenty-five euros. *"On y va."*

Nico follows her. Josie has taken charge of the tour now—Nico follows a half step behind. She pushes open the door of the salon, which is all bright lights and gleaming chrome surfaces with techno music pounding, and greets the young woman at the desk. The woman's hair is chartreuse and spiky. Maybe this isn't the place to get a grown-up haircut after all.

"I'd like a cut," Josie tells the woman in French. "I don't have an appointment."

"I can do it," the young woman says, and Josie wonders for a brief moment if she's really a stylist or if everyone's out to lunch and the assistant wants to make some extra money on the side.

But soon enough Josie is draped in a robe, her hair is washed and combed, and she's staring at herself in the mirror. She sees Nico standing behind her. The stylist asks what she wants and the music pounds in Josie's ears.

"I want to look older and wiser," Josie says. "I want to look like someone with a job and a boyfriend and a house in the country."

"Non," the woman says. *"C'est pas possible."*

Josie looks at Nico as if she needs a translation. He shrugs. The woman starts cutting.

"Wait," Josie says. "What are you going to do?"

"I will make you look like a movie star."

"I don't want to look like a movie star."

All the while the woman's fingers move at the speed of light and the *click-click-click* of the scissors reverberates in Josie's ears. Hair drops to the floor in long clumps.

"Everyone wants to look like a movie star."

"Which movie star?" Josie says weakly. She's feeling nauseated again and this time it has nothing to do with the pregnancy.

"Where are you from?" the woman asks.

"The United States."

"You speak French. Americans don't speak French."

"Some of us do."

"There is an American movie star filming in Paris today. On the Pont des Arts in about an hour. We're closing the shop soon. My receptionist already left to get a good spot."

"Who is it?" Josie asks.

"Dana Hurley. She is incredibly sexy, no?"

"You're cutting too much hair," Nico tells the stylist.

"Who are you? The boyfriend?"

"No," Josie says.

"Yes," Nico says.

Josie glares at him.

"Alors," the stylist tells Josie.

Josie closes her eyes and feels the young woman's hands ruffle her hair. She feels light, weightless, as if she might float away.

"Does Dana Hurley have short hair?" she asks, her eyes still closed.

"Yes," the stylist says. "Oh, I don't know. They change their hair so often. In her last film she had a bob. It doesn't matter what she does with her hair—she is someone I want to fuck."

"She's old, isn't she?" Nico asks.

Josie hears them as if they're far away. With her eyes closed and the snip of the scissors in her ear, the pounding of the techno-pop in her bones, the sensation of air on her neck, she feels transported somehow. Maybe she's on her way to becoming someone else.

"Oh, she must be forty-five or so, but she is the woman we all want to be. She is sexy and passionate and good in her skin. You know what I mean?"

Bien dans sa peau. Good in her skin, Josie thinks. I haven't been good in my skin since the last night I spent with Simon.

"I don't know," Nico says. "I've never gone for the older woman thing."

"That's because most older women lose something," the stylist says. "They lose their fuckability. They stop thinking about sex all the time and they think about jobs and country houses."

Josie opens her eyes. She sees someone else in the mirror. Her hair frames her face and her eyes look wide, her mouth looks full. She looks older and younger—she looks wild and she doesn't look scared.

"Oui, chérie?" the stylist says, leaning close. "See what I mean? You are a movie star, no?"

She was grading papers in her cottage late at night when the doorbell rang. She opened the door and saw Simon standing there in the porch light, his hair tousled, his dress shirt untucked from his pants. He looked at her, his expression dark and unfamiliar.

"What's wrong?" she said.

He stepped in and pulled the door closed behind him. He pushed her up against the wall and pressed his mouth on hers.

His kiss was hard and insistent. He pushed his leg between her legs and she could feel the weight of him against her.

When his mouth moved away from hers he made a noise, something low and guttural.

He took both her hands in one of his and held them above

her head, pressed hard against the wall. She heard her own voice say his name. His other hand slid under the band of her pajama bottoms and rubbed against her, urgently, while his leg pushed her legs farther apart. She was wet, and when she started to say something only a noise escaped her mouth and again his mouth was on hers.

He pushed her pajamas down and they tangled at her feet. She heard his hand pull at his belt, at the fly, and he lifted her up and she wrapped her legs around him and then he was inside her. He released her hands and she wrapped them around his back while he pressed her hard against the wall, each thrust pounding her back, pushing them closer. A painting on the wall rattled. She could feel him deep inside her and she wanted even more of him.

"Don't stop," she managed to say when he started to come and his orgasm kept rolling and their bodies, now slick with sweat, kept pounding together against the wall.

When he was done, he held her for a moment, and their hearts beat furiously against each other. They stepped out of their pants and he carried her to the bedroom, laid her down, and buried his face between her legs. She pressed the back of his head, arched her back, and came in waves that rolled on top of one another.

And then he was inside her again. He was still hard, but he held her still and they didn't move, their bodies wet and trembling.

She waited for a long time. *Stay with me,* Josie thought.

When he pulled out of her he looked at her and smiled— a sweet, exhausted grin.

His breath slowed. He ran his fingers over her stomach, her hips.

"Look at you," he said. His voice sounded sad and lost.

His fingers moved to her breasts, massaging them and then teasing her nipples.

"You're so young," he said. "So impossibly young."

Josie reached out and touched his face, ran her finger along his jaw.

"Don't get all old man on me," she teased.

"I can forget about youth," Simon said, his voice quiet and serious. "I mean, I see it all the time—in movies, in ads, young men and women and their firm bodies, their smooth skin. But my own youth slips away, not noticeably, not enough to terrify me, until one day I end up in bed with a beautiful young woman. And then all at once, I'm an old man."

They looked at each other, their faces close together on the bed, their hands both resting on each other's hips.

"Is that it—your age? That's what's upsetting you?" she asked.

He winced, then closed his eyes. When he opened them again, he looked terribly sad.

"I'm a good man," he said.

"I know that."

"I never meant to do this to my wife."

"Did she—"

"No, she doesn't suspect. She wouldn't suspect."

He stopped and she waited for him to finish. She brushed his hair back from his forehead.

"It's not an affair," he said.

"What is it?"

"I'm too old to start over."

"I'm not asking you to start over."

"But I can't give myself to you."

"You give yourself to me every time we're together."

He touched her lips with his fingers.

"No, it's not that," he said, shaking his head. "It's that I can no longer give myself to her."

He looked close to tears. He looked like someone else, like someone she'd never seen before.

"You're so fucking young," he said.

"Why does that matter?" she asked.

"My wife. Now, every time I look at her, I see—"

"No, don't. I don't want to blame myself for that."

"It's not your fault."

"Don't compare us. That's not fair."

"I can't leave you behind. You're with me all the time."

He pulled her to him and they held each other.

"How long does it take for hair to grow?" Nico asks. He looks like a frightened boy.

"Oh, don't be foolish. This is great. This is just what I wanted if only I had known what I wanted. I needed a lesbian to unleash me."

"Turn around," he says.

He spins Josie around, in the middle of the sidewalk, and a few people stop to stare. They all smile, as if they too are pleased with the tousled hair, the shy smile, the adoring young man.

"*Bon,*" Nico says decisively. "I still love you."

"Don't talk about love," Josie says. "You're not in love with me."

Nico leans over and kisses Josie on the mouth. She steps back, her mouth open in a small O of surprise. Nico smiles and turns away from her.

"Follow me," he says.

She stays where she is. People pass her on the street. She watches Nico walk jauntily ahead. She remembers the last time she saw Simon. "Wait for me," he had said. He had kissed her, standing on her porch, more daring in the light of day than he'd ever been. She had watched him walk away, down the long, sun-drenched street toward his car. His body disappeared into the harsh glare of sunlight until her eyes burned with the strain of keeping him in sight. He was gone. Still she stood there, feeling his mouth on hers. *Wait for me.*

"Are you coming?" Nico calls from the corner.

She shakes her head. She watches him walk back toward her.

"Don't be mad," he says sweetly. "I had to do it."

"He's gone," Josie says.

"Your lover?"

"I can't show him my new haircut."

Nico waits quietly for the rest.

"I can't say goodbye."

Nico puts his hand on her arm. "You are saying goodbye."

Josie shakes her head and her hair tousles, then settles again. "You know what he taught me? He taught me to feel more. He taught me to give myself over to feelings. And now that's all I have. I'm swamped by them. I can't breathe because I feel so damn much."

Nico takes her arm and leads her down the street. They walk for a long time. Finally they come to the end of a small street and ahead of them is an open stretch of lawn.

"I know where we are," Josie says.

She looks down the stretch of grass and there sits the Eiffel Tower. It's grand, majestic. It doesn't matter how many times Josie has seen it, each time it takes her breath away.

"Let's go," Nico says, and Josie knows exactly what he has in mind.

Brady knocked on Josie's office door even though it was open.

"Hey, you," Josie said.

She stretched out a hand, offering him a seat across from her. She was reading a contemporary French novel that she had thought she might teach next semester. She wanted something new, something the kids would relate to. She already knew that the story was too adult for her kids, too racy and full of sex scenes that they would undoubtedly love, and that would get her into a ton of trouble, but she kept reading.

"Am I disturbing you?" Brady asked.

"No, not at all." She put the book on her desk, cover down, as if she had been doing something illicit. "What's up?"

"I was wondering . . ." Brady looked around the room, at the photos on her wall—photos she had taken of the creek behind her cottage—at the stack of books on the floor, and out the window where the rest of the students were piling into cars and heading home.

In the silence she watched him. He had Simon's startling green eyes, Simon's thick, wavy hair, Simon's height. In the small room she realized that he smelled like Simon and she pushed the thought away. Of course, she thought. They use the same soap.

"My dad wants me to do the regular college thing. You know, liberal arts. Like everyone else in the world. That's what I always thought I'd do. I mean, I never really thought about it, but now, I'm like a junior and I have to think about these things."

It all came out in a breathless rush, as if he couldn't stop himself.

"What do *you* want, Brady?" Josie asked.

"Well, that's it. That's what I was wondering. I mean, this is completely crazy, but I really loved doing the play. It's like I was someone else up there and I get it. I really get how actors inhabit other people, like they give themselves up and they live in someone else's body for a while. And this is the wild part, the part that I never would have figured out except it happened to me. When the play is over and you go back to being you again, you're like a different you. You're changed. It's like you're not the guy you played onstage, but you take a little bit of him back with you."

He took a deep breath.

"You think I'm nuts, right?"

"No. I think you're very smart."

"Really? Cool. I've been thinking about this and I didn't really know if I could explain it or anything. And then if I could, like, who would I tell."

"Me."

"Yeah. You get it, huh? That's really cool."

His smile was huge and he sat on the edge of his seat, his legs jangly, his fingers tapping on his knees.

"And the school thing?" Josie asked, though she already knew everything he was about to say.

"I could go to acting school. I could apply to UCLA Drama School and USC and the Tisch program at NYU, and I got all the catalogs and I read them before I go to sleep at night and then I can't sleep, I'm so jazzed about this stuff. You should read what they say. I mean, it's all about the stuff you talked about when we started the play. About searching within to find what you can bring to the part. About learning your character like you're learning to breathe in a brand-new way."

He stood up and walked to one of the photos on the wall.

"This is cool. This is really great. You took these?"

"Yeah. Last summer."

"You're great. You're like the best teacher here."

He swung around and looked at her and then dropped back into the chair.

"You gotta talk to my dad."

"I don't think so, Brady."

"Yeah. You'd be so good at it. He'd listen to you. He's not listening to me."

"It's not my job."

"All you gotta do is tell him that I'm good enough. I'm good enough, right?"

She looked at him and saw that he was terrified in that moment, that he had no idea if he was good enough.

"You're good enough, Brady," she said.

He shot up out of his chair again. "So you gotta talk to him. Tell him that. Tell him lots of smart kids go to drama school."

"I don't know, Brady," Josie said. "It's not such a bad idea. What your dad wants. You can study acting later."

"But it's all I care about!" he shouted. "Don't you get it? I thought you'd get it. I thought you'd help me out here."

"I'll talk to him," she said quietly.

"Soon," he said. "We're flying down to look at schools next weekend. He's like all fired up about this. Father-son bonding time. He was never around and now he's my best fucking friend."

...

Nico and Josie start to climb. The stairs of the tower wind around the inside of one of the legs, the Pilier Est. Josie feels like she's in the belly of a giant erector set. It is hard work—Josie is glad that the stairs only go to the second level—after that, they have to take the elevator like everyone else. They're alone in this maze of steel. At one point a young boy sprints past them, as if shot from a cannon below. Suddenly Josie feels old. How can that kid dash up these stairs? Wasn't she young and fit about three weeks ago?

Josie catches glimpses of the city through the ironwork of the tower's leg, a peek of the meandering River Seine on one side, the grassy stretch of the Champ de Mars on the other. She has no fear of heights; she is not the little girl in her story. She has lost her mother, but she sure as hell doesn't expect to find her waiting at the top of the tower. Her father, though, might just be waiting for her, perched in the window of her childhood house, the chandelier lit above him, staring out into the street. He is waiting for Josie to come home. Maybe she'll bring a nice young man with her, a boyfriend. That's all he wants.

This is ridiculous, Josie thinks. Nico has invented some kind of therapy for her, some way for her to exorcize her grief while exercising her legs. Fine. At least they've stopped talking. At least he's stopped staring at her like a hungry puppy.

At least she's still wearing her sneakers and not some ridiculous pair of stiletto heels.

Nico is a few steps ahead of her, climbing steadily. Next she'll find out he's an Olympic athlete in his spare time. *Odd*, she thinks. She knows nothing about him. Why is he a tutor? Is that a career choice or something to do while writing poems? She used to be someone who was curious about people. She'd collect life stories from strangers on planes and buses. Now she talks to no one. And finally, here she is, spending a day with someone, and she's learned so little about him. He loves another French tutor. He hid in the root cellar as a child. He has a child in Morocco. Who is he? Has he really fallen for her or is this his charming way to teach a foolish American girl? And why the hell is she following him to the top of the tower?

She tries to quiet the sound of her own ragged breath. It's been too long since she hiked in the hills or biked out into the country. Since Simon. She's lost her ability to breathe since Simon.

"What will we do in Paris once we've bought your new shoes?" Simon had asked.

She was the pro, the French speaker. He had traveled to Paris on business once or twice but knew nothing of the city. Had he been to the Eiffel Tower? Probably not. And, of course, now she'd never know.

"We'll do the same thing we do here," she had told him.

"Wrong," Simon said, smiling. "We'll drag our sorry asses out of bed and see the city. I want to walk every street of the city with you on my arm."

It was going to be their first trip together, their first chance to go to sleep together and wake up together for six straight days.

"One more floor," Nico calls out like a personal trainer urging her on to seventy-three more push-ups. Now the sky takes up more space, the river snakes longer and narrower, and the houses become rooftops, blending into one another.

Josie sees that the skies are darkening, and a cold breeze passes through. She can feel the wind on her neck and she remembers her haircut. She lifts her hand and runs it through her hair. He'll never see it, she thinks.

"It's not working," she calls out to Nico.

"What's not working?"

"Isn't this your cure? Shouldn't I be feeling better already?"

"Keep climbing," he calls back.

Josie feels perspiration in the small of her back. She rolls her tank top up and wipes the sweat away. Then her hand snakes around to her belly, and she holds it there. It's flat, it's taut, it feels the same way it's always felt. But she's pregnant, she knows it. She had gone off the pill and Simon had started to use condoms. Did they ever forget?

The day in the rowboat. They weren't thinking of condoms; they were thinking about the depth of the lake, the iciness of the water, the rockiness of the boat. They were risking his marriage, her job, his relationship with his son, her relationship with her father.

They never thought about the other risk they took.

Simon's gone, Brady's gone. She holds her hands over her belly and climbs the stairs.

"I have never been to the top of the tower," Nico calls back.

"Are you afraid?" Josie asks.

"Of heights? No. Of love. Perhaps."

"Is this about love?"

"Every French man and woman either loves the tower or hates the tower. You can't ignore it. It's here, blocking our view or gracing our view, every day. It doesn't matter where you are. The tower is always there."

"Do you love it or hate it?"

"Today I will decide," Nico says.

Josie feels lighter on her feet. Somehow she has a second wind and the steps seem easier to scale. There is more air, a lighter breeze passing through. She loves the feeling of air on her neck.

"Today I will decide," she calls up to Nico.

"About the tower?"

"About Provence," she says. "Whether I will lose my mind completely and run off with my tutor."

"This is a good place to lose one's mind," Nico tells her.

They met in a motel off Highway 101, a half hour from their homes. It was a little dangerous—Simon told her he didn't have time for a long drive. He was getting sloppy. He had called her from his house a few days before, late at night, when his wife was sleeping. Ten minutes into the conversation, they heard a click and then Brady's voice, "Hello? Dad? You on the phone?"

"I'll be off in a second."

"It's one in the morning."

"Brady, go back to bed. I'll be up soon."

"Who you talking to?"

"Germany. It's a business call. Please don't interrupt us any more than you have."

Brady slammed the phone down.

This time Simon said, "I won't know anyone there. It's a dive. I need to see you."

"I know people who stay at dives," Josie said.

"Please, Josie. I have something to give you."

She called off a meeting with the Honor Society, which was planning a graduation tea.

"We only have a week till graduation," Alicia Loy whined. "We have to meet now."

"Alicia, it's a damn tea," Josie said, regretting it the minute the words were out of her mouth. "I can't do it. I told you. I have an emergency."

She arrived at the motel. It was worse than a dive—it looked abandoned and ready for demolition. She parked next to Simon's Audi and knocked on the only room that was lit.

He opened the door and pulled her in, closing the door behind her.

"Don't breathe," he said. "It smells like someone died in here."

"How romantic."

He held her pressed against him, her back to his chest. He lowered his head and kissed the top of her head.

"On the bed," he whispered, "is a gift."

She looked at the wool blanket, the gray sheets, the lumpy pillows. She could see where the bed sagged in the middle.

"Under the bed," she whispered, "is a dead body."

"It only smells that way," Simon told her. "I checked."

"I don't see your gift."

"It's where gifts always are: under the pillow."

She turned in his arms and kissed him.

"If I stay really close to you," she murmured, "then I can only smell you. And you smell wonderful."

"Go get your gift."

She pulled back and looked at him. He looked boyish in his pleasure.

She walked to the bed and lifted the closest pillow. An enve-

lope. She reached for it and glanced at the front. A drawing of
the Eiffel Tower. A good drawing, with an artistic flair.

"Did you draw this?" she asked.

"One of my many talents. And you thought I was only a
good lay."

"Wow," she said. "An artist."

"A French artist."

"Drawing the Eiffel Tower doesn't make you a French artist,
my love."

"Open the envelope."

She did. Inside were two business-class plane tickets to Paris.
She turned toward him, her eyes wide.

"You can do this?"

"I can do this."

"How?"

"A business trip. It doesn't matter. We leave the day school
ends for you."

"I have teacher meetings. No—yes. I'll cancel everything.
We're going to Paris!"

She threw herself into his arms.

"You'll help me find a hotel. I didn't know which neighborhood, I didn't know whether you would want something grand
or something intimate. I want to know all these things about
you. I want to eat in wonderful restaurants without worrying
about who will see us."

"I'll teach you French. We'll talk dirty in French in bed with
each other."

"I'm terrible at languages."

"I'll be your French tutor."

"You don't talk dirty in English."

"That's just because I can't catch my breath."

"Say 'Undress me' in French."

"*Déshabille-moi.*"

"Say 'Fuck me.'"

"*Baise-moi.*"

"Say 'Devour me.'"

"*Dévore-moi.*"

"Say 'Don't ever stop.'"

"*N'arrête jamais.*"

"Say you'll come with me to Paris."

"*Je t'aime.*"

Nico and Josie reach the top of the tower. Josie takes a deep breath and finally allows herself to look out. She was glad for the elevator ride, but she kept her eyes closed as she was whisked to the top.

Now she looks out, way out. The observation tower is crowded with people who all seem to be speaking at once— a jumble of languages and sounds. She walks slowly, unsteadily, to one window. She feels as if she's not yet landed, that her legs need to keep climbing. She's got sea legs, miles above the sea.

When she reaches the window she takes in a lungful of air and then holds it. It's as if she doesn't want to let go of what she sees. All of Paris is spread before her, from the heights of Sacré-Coeur, down along the banks of the Seine, out to the farthest reaches of each arrondissement. The clouds swirl around her, at eye level, and every once in a while the city disappears and she's heaven-bound. Then a gust of wind pushes away the cloud and, like magic, Paris sits at her feet.

She looks straight out into the sky and sees what Simon must have seen in his small plane. Clouds, sky, space. It's enormous and infinite and thrilling.

"Take me," she had said when he told her how he loved to fly.

Now she knows. Now she has a piece of him that was missing. He loved this: the wild space of it, the changing possibility of clouds and sky, the power of height.

"Thank you," she says to Nico when he comes to her side.

He stands next to her for a long while, both of them silent, both gazing out into the sky.

Josie remembers the weight of Simon's body after they would make love. They would fall into each other, wrapping themselves as closely into each other's bodies as possible. "Come closer," he would say. "Yes," she would say. After losing themselves during sex, they would land, and they needed to take away all the space between them.

Did he die in the sky? Did something happen in the plane while it flew through the sky? Is this what he saw before he died? Or did he come to earth and die when the plane crashed into the hard, unyielding ground? Did he and Brady know they were going to die? Did they hold each other and wait for it to happen?

"Take me," she had said to Simon.

He left without taking her.

She makes a sound and Nico puts his arm around her.

The clouds move in and surround them. They can no longer see the city below. They're wrapped in silvery black clouds, cocooned in space.

"I love it," Nico says finally. "My tower. My Paris."

. . .

Simon had said he'd come over to Josie's cottage after dinner. He told his wife another client was in town, that once again he needed to stop by the guy's hotel to buy him a drink and talk up tomorrow's meeting. When the doorbell rang Josie thought Simon was early. She ran to the door, threw it open, and saw her father standing on the porch, flowers in his hand.

"Dad!"

"I'm disturbing you?"

"No, of course not. I'm just surprised."

"Your old man was in the neighborhood."

She ran dates through her mind—it wasn't her mother's birthday, their anniversary, the anniversary of her death.

"You don't need an excuse," she said. "Come have dinner with me."

"Dinner? I don't need dinner. I just need a little time with my girl."

"I'm eating, Dad. You want time with me, you have to eat, too."

She stepped aside and let him pass. He clung to his flowers as if he had no intention of giving them to her.

"Smells good in here," he said, heading straight to the kitchen.

"I gotta make a call, Dad. Pour yourself a glass of wine. I'll throw in the pasta in a second."

"Pasta. Wine. I should come more often."

She smiled and kissed him. He seemed smaller. No, she was used to standing on tiptoe to kiss Simon.

She walked into her bedroom and closed the door. She had to reach Simon, to tell him not to come. He'd be home, having dinner with his wife and Brady. She'd call on his cell phone but still, it was risky. She had to do it—she didn't want him showing up with her dad here.

She dialed his number. It rang and rang. She hung up and texted him: *Call me.*

They were careful about text messages—too easy for his wife to pick up the phone and find the revealing words.

She waited a few minutes, pacing in her room. It was rude to leave her dad alone after he had driven all this way. Simon was probably in the middle of dinner. She'd try him again later.

She found her dad in the kitchen looking for a vase.

"Up here," she told him, and reached above the refrigerator for the tall glass cylinder. "They're beautiful." Blue irises. Her mother loved irises. Again Josie tried to remember what day it might be—not Mother's Day or her father's birthday. Something made him get in the car and drive an hour and a half to drop in. She didn't have a clue.

She took the flowers and placed them in the vase, filled it with water. She set the vase on the windowsill, next to her kitchen table. "Nice," she said, pleased. "You've never brought me flowers."

"Someone should spoil you," he said.

The phone rang. She leapt at it.

"Hey, you," Simon whispered in her ear.

"Mr. Reed. Thanks for calling me back. I need to talk to you about your son's college choices. He and I met a few days ago and I promised I'd chat with you."

"Well, thank you, Ms. Felton. Very responsible of you."

"But my father just dropped in for a visit. Let's talk about this another time?"

"You go ahead," her father insisted. "I can wait."

She shook her head. Now there would be no reason to take the phone into the other room. She was caught in her lie.

"Why don't we talk about it during the parent-teacher conference tomorrow," Josie said into the phone. "What time are you coming by? I have it written somewhere—"

"Can you go home for lunch?" Simon whispered. "I'll stop by then. Brady and I fly out at three."

"Noon it is, then. Thanks very much, Mr. Reed."

She hung up the phone.

"You're very good at what you do," her father said. "It seems like it wasn't very long ago that I might have been having that conversation with one of your teachers."

No, Josie thought. You would never have had that conversation.

She walked over and kissed him again.

"Thanks for coming, Dad. I've missed you."

"You could visit once in a while. It wouldn't kill you."

"I have so much work on the weekends."

"You bring it with you. I can cook you a dinner once in a while. Where's that wine? I couldn't find it."

Josie found a bottle of wine in her cupboard and opened it. Her father never would have had an affair. He was such a good husband, such a loyal man. But Simon had told her that he had never imagined that he would slip out the back door and take another woman to bed. "I'm a good man," he had told her. Had he stopped being a good man when he fell in love with her?

She poured wine into their glasses. She handed her father a glass and took a sip of hers. An evening with her dad instead of her lover. She wasn't disappointed. It was a chance to catch her breath.

"Sit down and let me get this meal together," she told him.

He sat at the table and watched her. She put the pasta in the boiling water, then set the small table. She already had the sauce made—a simple tomato sauce with herbs from her garden. She tossed the salad with some vinaigrette.

"Look at you," her dad said. "You would have made your mom proud."

Josie smiled. She had often thought of that: *Mom should see me cook. Mom should see me teach.* But when she began her affair with Simon she no longer wished her mother alive to watch over her. When she thought about her mother now, she felt a hot blast of shame.

"Tell me what's new, Dad. How's the store?"

"Same old," he said. "Nothing changes anymore. One of these days I'll sell out and move to Palm Springs."

"No you won't," Josie said. "You'd leave me?"

"Maybe you'll visit more in Palm Springs."

"Hey, guess what. I'm going to Paris!"

The timer rang and she tested the pasta, then poured it into the colander. She heated it with the sauce for a moment while she concocted her lie.

"You remember Whitney? My friend from college? We're going together for six days."

"You can afford something like that on your teacher's salary?"

"Whitney got a great deal. I'm really happy about it. Paris!"

"Yeah. Good for you, Josie. You bring me back one of those berets the old men wear. I'd look good in one of those."

Josie smiled. "You'd look great in one of those."

She served them and sat across from her father.

"You really going to move to Palm Springs?"

"Who knows? I'm thinking about it. There's a lady I know who's got a place down there. She wants me to visit."

"A lady?"

"You never heard of a lady before?"

"A girlfriend lady?"

"It's not impossible."

"Dad. That's great. Since when?"

"Since never. I said it's not impossible."

"Tell me about the lady."

"Somebody I met at bridge. A nice lady."

"I'm glad, Dad. I'm really glad."

"So what's wrong with you? Your old man can meet a lady and you can't bring home a boyfriend?"

"I'll bring home a boyfriend, Dad. I promise."

"Yeah?"

"I don't know. It's very complicated. There's a man I like. I don't know."

"What's not to know?"

"Like I said, it's complicated."

Her father put his wineglass down on the table. He pushed his chair back and stood up.

"He's married," he said, his voice low.

"I didn't say that."

"Love isn't complicated. Married men are complicated."

"Forget I said anything."

"Your mother would be very upset with you."

"Don't bring her into this."

"I'm not hungry."

"Dad. Sit down."

Her father walked into the other room. Josie was furious with herself for saying something—there was no reason to talk about Simon. She got up and followed her father into the living room.

He was standing by the front door as if considering his escape. He gazed through the window; his face was dark and brooding.

"This is the day your mother was diagnosed," he said quietly, as if he weren't even talking to her. "Eight years ago."

"Oh," Josie said weakly. She stood back, scared that if she went to him, he'd throw open the door and disappear.

"I went with her to the doctor's appointment. We thought it was nothing—some swelling in her ankles, a little discomfort, nothing important. But you know how much she hated the doctor."

His hands hung limply at his sides. He looked helpless, lost, as if what happened eight years ago happened over and over again.

"She went in to the appointment and I stayed in the waiting room with all the ladies. Then the nurse came into the room and said, 'The doctor will meet with you now.' I knew everything I needed to know right then. I didn't need him to say a word."

"How was Mom?" Josie asked.

"Quiet. Scared. We sat in front of the doc's desk in his fancy office and listened to him talk about surgery and chemo and new kinds of treatment. But right then I knew: I had lost her. I lost my world. I lost my life."

There were tears running down his face. Josie swiped at her own face with the back of her hand.

"I'm sorry I was so far away," she said.

"Oh, you did what you needed to do. What all kids do. We never blamed you for that."

"Come have dinner with me, Dad."

"Eight years go by. And there's still all these feelings I have. Like I can't gather them up and put them away in a box."

Josie walked over to her father. He turned toward her and let her hold him.

After a moment he stepped away. "No married men," he said.

"Who said anything about a married man?" she told him.

Nico and Josie take the elevator down from the top of the Eiffel Tower.

"Let's walk along the Seine," Nico says.

"This is the first day I have spent back in the world," Josie tells him as they head toward the river. First they walk along the wide boulevard at the side of the road; below them, to their left, is the Seine and across it, the Grand Palais. Farther up is the Louvre. Then a stairwell takes them to a lower path, one that brushes the river and protects them from the street traffic and the mad crush of pedestrians.

"You have been hiding?"

"Hiding?" Josie says, considering the word. "No, there's no place to hide. I try the bed, with the covers pulled high, but even then, it finds me and knocks me out."

"Sadness?"

"I wish it were sadness. That seems kinder than what I feel now. It's a gut punch now. It's a wallop of grief."

"When your mother died . . . ?" Nico lets the question trail off. "I'm sorry," he says. "I'm asking too many questions."

"You are," Josie says. But she slides her hand around his arm and walks at his side with their arms linked together.

They're quiet for a while. The clouds have darkened the sky and they hear thunder far off in the distance.

"When my mother died," Josie says, "I remember thinking I was no longer a child. It all ended at once. I had just graduated from college, I was thousands of miles from home, and then she was gone. I floated for a while—it's so different. This grief has me crawling on the earth; that time I was cut loose and I couldn't ground myself. I had a lot of sex. Isn't that odd? I slept with every boy I knew—old friends, new friends, passing acquaintances. I guess I was trying to feel something. Now I feel too much."

"What happened?"

Josie looks at him, puzzled. "Oh, not much. I spent a year or two like that. And then I missed my father. All at once. I applied for every teaching job within a hundred miles of home. And I ended up in Marin. I never told him I came home to be with him."

"Why not?"

"Because once I got there, I rarely saw him."

Josie thought of her dad's last visit. They never talked about Simon again. They ate pasta and salad, they drank their wine in silence. After a while, he told a long story about two boys who tried to rob the grocery store but they got in a fight in the middle of the robbery. One boy punched the other, and they chased each other out of the store. Josie told her dad to sell the place; maybe Palm Springs was a good idea. It was so simple, sitting and sharing dinner with her father. When he got up to leave she said, "I'll come down next weekend." His face lit up.

And then Simon died. She called her father and told him she was sick in bed and couldn't travel.

"I'm tired of talking," Josie says to Nico, but she keeps her arm tucked around his. "Tell me about the woman you love. The other tutor."

"Did I mention her?"

"You did. You sleep with her but not with her boyfriend."

"Hmm. I must have had too much to drink at lunch."

"What is her name?"

"Chantal."

"A pretty name."

"A pretty woman. I only slept with her once. Though she's in my mind many nights when I go to bed."

"We imagine love so easily."

"Yes. That is the simple part."

"Does she love you?"

"She has a boyfriend, remember."

"Does she love her boyfriend?"

"I can't imagine. But then I don't understand women very well. He has a reputation of sorts. He's been known to sleep with his students."

"Not you," Josie says, smiling. "You wouldn't do a thing like that."

"I would not get so lucky," Nico says.

"But you were lucky enough to sleep with his girlfriend."

"Yes. Last week we all went out for a few drinks after work."

"You'll do that tonight?"

"Tonight I'm taking a train to Provence."

"Of course."

A *bateau-mouche* glides by on the river and they hear the loudspeaker barking out indecipherable words. They both turn to look. The tourists all seem to be looking at them: a couple strolling along the Seine. It should have been Simon, she thinks.

She takes her hand away from Nico's elbow and tucks her hands in her pockets.

"That night . . ." she says, prompting him. The boat passes by and they continue walking.

"That night Philippe was flirting with a girl at the café. She was sitting at a table nearby, with her dog at her feet, and he kept walking over and petting the dog. Finally he invited the girl to join us. For me, he said. So I wouldn't be so lonely. The girl and her dog moved to our table. I knew that Chantal was unhappy with Philippe; she is often unhappy with him. But she usually goes home with him at the end of each evening. I don't under-stand her."

"But you love her."

"Oh, I don't know if I love her. She's beautiful in a very seri-ous way. Not like you."

"I'm beautiful in a silly way."

"Not at all. Even now, you have something so alive in you."

"Even now."

"You will come through this."

"You're very kind. And you're off the subject. Chantal."

"Yes," Nico says. "Chantal was angry. She doesn't show her emotions very easily. But I watch her face and I see how it changes."

"I like you, Nico."

He stops walking and looks at Josie.

"No kissing," she says. "Keep walking and keep talking."

"Chantal doesn't like dogs. The girl's little dog climbed up on Philippe's lap and sat there looking very smug."

"And the girl?"

"She was loud. She told a bawdy story about getting a lap dance from a stripper in a club the night before. Philippe asked

her if she likes girls, and she said she likes girls and boys and foreigners. She especially likes foreigners."

"Charming."

"Chantal asked me to walk her home. Philippe was supposed
to say no, that he would take her. Philippe was too busy having
his fingers licked by the awful dog."

"You walked her home."

"I walked her right into bed. It was revenge sex. But when we
were done Chantal asked me not to tell Philippe."

"So why did she sleep with you?"

"To prove that she didn't care about the girl and her dog."

"Does she know that you love her?"

"No—yes. I don't know what I feel. How could she know
what I feel?"

"Sometimes women are better at this than men."

"True," Nico says. "If I meet her for a drink tonight she'll tell
me if I love her. But if I go with you to Provence, I'll never
know."

"You deserve love," Josie tells him.

Nico looks at her and she sees that his face is open with hope.

"Look," Josie says, pointing ahead. "The film shoot that the
hairstylist told us about."

They can see a mass of people ahead, spread across both
sides of the river. On the Pont des Arts, an iron pedestrian
bridge that crosses the Seine from the Institut Français on the
Left Bank to the Louvre on the Right Bank, there are cameras
and lights and a couple of tents set up at the far side.

"Let's go watch," Josie tells him, her voice excited.

"Why is everyone so starstruck?" Nico asks, holding back.

Josie takes his hand and pulls him forward. "Oh, come on.
We need our movie stars. We need the big screen."

"Why? Why is that any more important than this? Because it has bright lights and cameras?"

"Because it's bigger than we are. We disappear. This day? Tomorrow it's gone. But that—that might be a day on the Seine that happens over and over for a hundred years."

After the funeral—with the two matching caskets—after Josie left the hundreds of students and parents and friends and relatives and drove herself home, she lowered the shades in her cottage and crawled into bed. She took a sleeping pill and sometime in the middle of a dreamless sleep, the phone rang.

Before she thought better, she reached over to her bedside table and answered it.

"You okay?" It was Whitney again. After months of silence, Whitney was back. The married boyfriend was gone.

"I can't talk, Whitney. I'm sleeping."

"Don't talk. Listen."

"I don't want to listen."

"This is for the better—"

"Fuck off, Whitney."

"I don't mean his death. That's tragic. And his son. I can't believe it."

Josie hung up the phone. Her mouth was dry and there was no water left in the glass by her bed. She pushed herself up and out of bed. She was sweaty from sleeping under too many covers. She threw off her clothes and when she glanced in the mirror she saw her body, the body that Simon made love to over and over again. She turned away, found fresh pajamas, and covered herself in them.

She shuffled to the kitchen and poured a glass of water.

The window was filled with late-evening light and her father's blue irises. She had forgotten to move them and lower the shade. She dropped into the seat and gazed at the flowers. Then behind them, through the window, she saw a deer. It looked at her and tilted its head to one side. Then it turned away, and in one graceful leap, it crossed the creek and disappeared into the woods.

I want to leave, Josie thought. I want to flee.

She walked to the phone and picked it up. She called her boss, the head of the school, at her home.

"Did you go to the funeral?" Stella asked. "There were so many people there. I didn't see you."

"I was there," Josie said.

"That poor woman," Stella muttered.

"Listen," Josie said. "This might be bad timing. But I wanted to tell you that I won't be back next year."

"Let's talk about this on Monday, Josie."

"I have to do it now. I'll finish up classes. But that's it."

"What are you planning to do?"

"I don't know," Josie said.

"You've been very distracted. Is something going on?"

Josie mumbled her goodbye and hung up.

She walked back into her bedroom. She was thankful for the darkness again. The room smelled rank. For a moment she remembered Simon's smell and she felt an ache in her chest. She covered her face with her hand and breathed in her own sour smell instead.

She walked to her dresser and picked up an envelope. She saw the drawing of the Eiffel Tower. At the top of the tower she saw two tiny figures. One had long hair; the other was very tall, with two green dots for eyes. She touched his mouth with her finger.

She opened the envelope. In two and a half weeks she would go to Paris. She didn't know what would happen after that. But for now, she had Paris to get her through her days.

Josie and Nico finally find a spot from which to watch the film shoot. Nico has led her to the top deck of a floating restaurant on the edge of the quai. It's a long boat, with beautiful teak floors and deck chairs and white umbrellas. There's a bar at the far end of the boat, crowded with people, all with drinks in hand. Josie and Nico squeeze past the crowd and lean against the railing with an unobstructed view of the bridge.

Next to them, a waiter has opened a bottle of champagne as if this were a premiere or a national event of great importance. He pours champagne, and the group—young office workers, perhaps, all escaping work to watch the filming—clink glasses.

"I'm not convinced that this is art that will last for a hundred years," Nico says.

A bed sits in the middle of the Pont des Arts. It's just a bed—a frame and mattress, thrown onto the wooden deck of the pedestrian bridge. A naked woman sprawls across the bed, on a rose-colored sheet. She's young and beautiful, and the enormous crowd on both sides of the river seems caught in a kind of reverential silence.

"Stop being a grump," Josie whispers. They are pressed together against the rail of the boat. "Isn't that Pascale Duclaux?" She points to a woman with a wild mess of red hair, perched in a chair at the edge of the set. "She's a very serious director. This may very well be great art."

"A bed on a bridge? A naked nymph?"

"And a man," Josie says. "Check out the old man."

A gray-haired man, also naked, circles the bed, his eye on the lovely girl. Dana Hurley, the American actress, stands at the edge of the bridge, her back against the rail, watching them. Unlike the other two, she's fully dressed. The man doesn't seem to notice her.

Then the man stops for a moment, his penis wagging between his legs, and he looks up, as if searching for something. He seems to catch Josie's eye and he holds it, a half smile on his face.

He's no older than Simon, Josie thinks. So why does it bother me so much that he's stalking this girl?

She looks away, breaking his stare. When she looks back, he resumes his awful walk, around the bed, as if roping the girl in.

The skies rumble and, in an instant, rain pours down. This part of the boat isn't covered—everyone turns and pushes back, under the white umbrellas or down below, under the deck. Josie stands there, watching the bridge, the bed, the girl, the man.

"Come on," Nico says. "This is crazy."

"Go ahead," she tells him. "I want to watch."

"There's nothing to watch. They're going to wait for the rain to stop."

But the director signals for the cameras to keep rolling.

Josie keeps her eye on Dana Hurley. Dana doesn't run. She's already soaked, her hair matted to her head. She walks toward the bed as if she doesn't have a care in the world. She won't lose her man to a young girl. She won't lose anyone to cancer or plane crashes. If something terrible happens the director will call "Cut!" and Dana will saunter back to her tent, where a fawning assistant will bring her a towel and a glass of champagne.

Josie realizes that Nico is right: This is not great art—this has nothing in it that will last longer than a day. The only thing that lasts is love, even when it's gone.

"Please," Nico says. "Come inside."

She turns to him. He is the nicest man she has ever met. For a moment she feels unburdened by grief. Even the sound of his voice offers something like hope. Yet she can't go to Provence with him. They are writing an ending to their own movie, a fairy-tale ending, and she no longer believes in fairy tales.

"I need to go back to my hotel," she tells him.

"Now?"

"I'll pack my bags," she lies. It is so much easier than saying goodbye. "I'll meet you at the train station at six."

His face lights up. Thunder crashes and, in an instant, lightning blasts through the gray skies and all of Paris shines in its glow.

Riley and Philippe

METRO
PALAIS-ROYAL

CAFÉ
MARLY

MUSÉE DU
LOUVRE

PONT
DES
ARTS

quai François Mitterrand

Quai des Grands Augustins

Seine R

Boulevard Saint-Germain

Boulevard de Sébastopol

rue Beaubourg

CENTRE
POMPIDOU

rue du Temple

rue de Rivoli

rue des Francs Bourgeois

Boulevard Beaumarchais

rue de Turenne

METRO
SAINT-PAUL

PLACE
DES
VOSGES

Voie Georges Pompidou

ÎLE
DE LA CITÉ

NOTRE
DAME

pont Saint-Louis

ÎLE
SAINT-LOUIS

Boulevard Henri IV

Quai de la Tournelle

She decides the minute she wakes up—with Cole pressed against her back, Gabi's tiny feet in her face, and Vic gone at some ungodly hour of the morning—that she will meet her French tutor somewhere else, anywhere else other than in this apartment. She usually has her lesson at her kitchen table. Today she needs to get out. She slides Gabi's feet—powdery-smelling baby feet—away from her and glances out the window. Rain. She hates Paris. It's the secret shame that she carries inside her. What the hell is wrong with her? Everyone loves this fucking city.

Riley has lived in Paris for a year, long enough—or so *every-one* says—to learn French, the métro system, and how to dress. She's a dismal failure. She should also have friends, cook souf-flés, and have the energy to have sex with her husband in the middle of the night. Except there are always children in her bed in the middle of the night, and she has no energy, day or night. But she's what her mother always called "a tough cookie," and so she tells no one that she's miserable. Besides, who would be-lieve her? She's living in Paris.

Here's what she has accomplished in a year in Paris:

1. She had a baby—no mean feat, since she never understood a word that the doctors and nurses at the clinic
   barked at her all day and night.
2. She has gained thirty-five pounds and lost twenty-five
   pounds and still eats a *pain au chocolat* every day, even
   though she can no longer blame it on the cravings of
   pregnancy.
3. She has learned where to buy paella at the street market
   near her home and serves it out of a bowl to the astonishment of Vic's co-workers.
4. She has lost contact with most of her old best friends
   from New York because she can no longer send them
   emails extolling the virtues of expat life.
5. She has convinced her mother—every day—not to visit.
   Yet.
6. She has watched two-and-a-half-year-old Cole learn
   French, make friends in the playground, lead her home
   when they are lost, and say the words, "It's okay,
   Mama," so many times that she worries that one day
   she'll murder someone and he'll pat her hand and say,
   "It's okay, Mama."
7. She has lost love. She had it when they moved here, and
   sometime during the first few weeks, while she and Vic
   were unpacking the dishes and books and Cole's toys,
   she misplaced it and hasn't been able to find it since.

Riley tries to maneuver her way out of bed without disturbing the kids, but they cling to her like vines. Take the tree
trunk away and those vines sink to the forest floor. In a quick
moment, Cole's asking questions: "Where's Daddy?" "What we
do today?" "Why rain, why rain?" and Gabi's crying, a whim-

pering, pitiful cry that probably means she's got another ear in-
fection.

Riley scoops Gabi into her arms and plops down in the arm-
chair, opens her pajama top, and attaches the baby to her breast.
Breathe, she tells herself. Breast-feeding is the one thing she
loves. She loves it so much that she does it far too much—she
knows what the baby books say about getting your child on a
schedule—but she just doesn't care. She wants only this: to sit in
her lemon-yellow overstuffed chair, as ugly as all the rest of the
mismatched items in this furnished apartment, and feel Gabi's
mouth on her breast, feel the comforting release of milk, and
pause.

Because in a minute she'll be moving again.

She'll call Philippe and tell him to meet her at a café.

She'll call Fadwa or Fawad or Fadul downstairs and ask her to
babysit. It's a school day. The girl won't be home. She'll ask the
girl's mother, but the woman doesn't speak English. She'll gesture: *Baby. Sit.* Like charades, she'll show the baby and then sit in
a chair. That's ridiculous. The word in Arabic probably doesn't
have anything to do with sitting.

Breathe, she tells herself.

"Why rain, why rain, why rain, why rain?" It's become a
chant as unnerving as a police siren, and Cole runs around the
house like he's on fire.

Riley looks at the clock. Seven-fifteen A.M. Where the hell is
Vic this early?

They fought last night, in the only time they spent together
before crawling, numb and exhausted, into bed. "You think I like
this life? You think I want to work all hours of the day and
night?"

"Yes," Riley said.

"That's ridiculous," Vic snapped. "I have to pull together a team from four different countries and most of them hate each other. I can barely understand half of them myself. You think I wouldn't rather build sand castles in the park in Place des Vosges?"

He was standing in the bathroom in his pajama bottoms, his bare belly gone soft and pale. He stabbed the air with his toothbrush like a fierce bathroom warrior. Riley looked at him and thought: Everything you say is the opposite. You love being the big shot who makes an international team work. You hate the sand.

"Get a grip, Riley," he said, spitting toothpaste into the sink.

And when did he start wearing pajama bottoms? Riley had a momentary wish to walk up to Vic and slide his pants down, wrap her body around her naked husband and whisper, "Come back to me." But he pushed past her and headed into the kitchen for another brownie, left over from a care package her mother sent a few days before.

Riley smells the top of Gabrielle's head. It's perfect baby smell and she remembers to breathe.

The phone rings and she jumps and Gabi's mouth pulls from her breast, taking her nipple with her. She screams and the baby cries. But the phone has stopped ringing. Then Cole walks in, carrying it. He's smiling. "Nana," he says.

He's never answered the phone before. She's amazed. Soon he'll put on a tie and leave for work at seven in the morning like all the other competent people in this household.

"Mom?" she says into the phone. She does a quick calculation—it's one in the morning in Florida.

Her mother is crying—or she's making a gulping sound of trying not to cry.

"What's wrong?"

She's not sentimental enough to be crying because her grandson answered the phone for the first time.

"Mom?"

"I don't want to bother you with this—"

"With what?"

"I didn't even want to tell you that I was having tests—"

And Riley knows everything she needs to know. Her father died of cancer years before, and somehow she waits for everyone she knows to get it and die. On TV, people survive; in her life, they die. She is crying, silently, a steady stream of wet stuff pouring down her face.

"Mama?" Cole asks.

"Mom?" Riley asks.

"Mama?"

"Shh, honey. I'm okay," Riley whispers. Or maybe that was her mother whispering to her. She's squeezing the baby too tightly.

"What tests?" she finally asks.

"Ovarian cancer."

"You should have told me."

"I'm telling you."

"I'm coming home."

"You're not coming home."

"Mom."

"Mama?" Cole is tapping her shoulder. She looks down. Gabi is hanging from one foot off her lap, ready to fall. How is it that Riley got a hold of this foot? And why is the baby laughing like this is some kind of game?

"Sorry, sweetie," Riley says, pulling Gabi back to safety. But there is no safety. Gabi throws up in Riley's lap.

"Mom, I'll call you back." And she hangs up.

She's holding Gabi in the air. Vomit puddles in her pajama bottoms. And Cole pats her shoulder. "It's okay, Mama."

Soon she will clean the mess and call her mother back.

Soon Cole will find a French cartoon on TV and watch happily as if he understands every single word of this damn language.

Soon she'll call Vic and ask him why he had to call a breakfast meeting when he had a dinner meeting last night and will have another dinner meeting tonight.

Soon she'll call every pediatrician listed in the guide her realtor gave her and ask every snooty receptionist, *"Parlez-vous anglais?"* until she finds someone who does, and she'll make an appointment to check Gabi's ears.

Soon it will stop raining.

Soon she'll see Philippe.

Riley slides into a chair inside the café—the rain has stopped for a moment, but she knows Paris well enough to know that the wet stuff will rain on her parade.

She's amazed she has managed so much already today. She called her mother back but Mom said she was going to sleep—it was 1:30 in the morning in Florida and she needed her beauty rest. Riley convinced the woman downstairs to watch the kids. She found clean clothes. They almost fit her—another ten pounds and she'll be back to her fighting weight. But she's not giving up the *pain au chocolat* and there is the problem of her enormous milk-laden breasts. *Tant pis.* She's learned that expression—too fucking bad. So the shirt pulls tight across her chest and the jeans hug her hips. *Tant pis,* Victor.

She's early. She opens her notebook to last week's lesson. The words swim in front of her eyes. She used to be a smart person. She used to be a person who had long conversations with intelligent people about politics and the arts and why her neighbor in apartment 3B sang in the middle of the night.

Now she's either silent or she talks to infants. Either way, there's been a diminishing of intelligence, she's noticed. Hard to discuss global warming when she's got potty mouth.

And Philippe won't speak English. She's sure he can—he's got that European *je ne sais quoi* that usually means "Oh, I speak six languages. And a little Japanese."

He thinks that if she has to speak in French, then she will. Instead, she sits there as if she's a timid soul, one of those mousy girls in high school who never raised her hand. "I'm the teacher's pet! she wants to scream. I've got so much to say that you can't shut me up!" But she has nothing to say, because she doesn't have any of the words with which to say it.

Her wondrous career, which she gave up three weeks before Cole was born—though she can't remember why anymore— had her writing crisis communications for major corporations. Stock tumbling? I'll spin that! CEO caught in the men's room with the mail boy? Give me a second and I'll explain how this is good for the company! But now she can't even turn her own life into a good story—because she doesn't have the words for it. *Je suis* lost.

The waiter comes over and asks her something that she knows she can answer. *"Café, s'il vous plaît."* Then he says something else and she nods. He's probably going to bring her a plate of pigs' feet with her coffee and she won't be able to complain. Because she doesn't have the words!

Six months ago, Cole went through a tough phase. Her American mom friends told her: "It's the terrible twos, don't worry, it will pass." He raged—throwing things, often including himself, onto the floor and most often in the most public places. She and Vic found a phrase that helped: "Use your words." And miraculously, as Cole learned his first few words, the tantrums stopped. He could say "Pop Tart" or "Rug Rat" or "Pig in Wig" or "bad Mama" and they would nod and get him what he needed. ("Bad Mama" meant that Daddy should put him to bed.) When Riley is standing in the middle of Les Enfants Rouges farmers' market and the cheese lady asks her something in rapid-fire French, Riley considers throwing herself on the ground and kicking her feet. *Use your words!* But there aren't any.

The waiter returns with coffee and no pigs' feet. Riley burns her tongue on the coffee. Doesn't matter, she thinks. Don't need this tongue. Everything about her feels raw. She has stopped crying and promised her mother she won't be a drama queen. It's only cancer, for Christ's sake. Everyone has cancer these days. Her mother is redefining "tough cookie" and Riley is re-defining ball of mush. "On with your day!" her mother ordered. This is her day then. On with it!

She looks around the café. The place is crowded though it's mid-morning. Is Vic the only one who goes to work in this city? Everyone else seems to sit in cafés all day, drinking endless espresso until they start drinking wine. They're immaculately dressed, as if eventually they'll either go to the office or a movie premiere. One woman is wearing a leopard suit, skintight, with four-inch stilettos. Probably on her way to pick up her babies and go to the park, Riley thinks.

The door opens and Philippe breezes in.

He's tall and gangly and has wasted-rock-star good looks. Too many drugs, too many hard nights. It becomes him. His hair always falls in his eyes and Riley spends much of the French lessons imagining something so simple: She reaches out and tucks that lovely hair behind his ear. Today it's a little greasy, though. Maybe she'll pay better attention to the lesson.

"Je suis désolé," he says breathlessly. She smells cigarettes and coffee and something else—sex? His clothes are rumpled. Did he rush here from his girlfriend's bed?

She smiles at him. She could say something like "No big deal," or "What is that delicious smell wafting from you?" but she doesn't have the words.

When he had answered his cell phone earlier she had started to speak in English. *"En français,"* he admonished her. And so she gave him the name and address of the café and a time. That's all. She felt a little bit like a spy giving out only the crucial information. No chitchat for her. She's got international intrigue on her mind!

"Bon," he says, settling into the seat across from her, pulling out his books from his very distressed leather messenger bag, ordering something from the waiter who says something in response, and then he turns to her and smiles.

She smiles back.

He asks a question.

She smiles back.

He shakes his head, unleashing that lock of hair. She looks away.

"Bon," he says again. Though nothing is good. Even the coffee tastes like burnt tongue.

"Okay, listen," she says in English. "Maybe we try something different. Maybe we get to know each other a little bit, figure out something we'd both like to talk about—I mean, I don't know a thing about you—and then we could, I don't know, talk about that. In English. And then eventually I'd be speaking in French because it would be just so interesting that the French words would squeeze their way into my little brain and pour right out of my mouth. Whaddaya think?"

"*En français,*" he says. He's smiling though. Either he's a nice guy or he understood every word she said.

That's the other thing. She doesn't know how to read people here. Back in the States, she had a sharp ear—she could figure out who was worth knowing by how they spoke, how witty they were, how observant and caustic and wry. She chose her best friend because the woman used remarkable metaphors, inventing them on the spot. She chose her first boyfriend because he skewered the sociology professor for his foppish mannerisms. She chose her husband because he was the first guy to beat her at Scrabble. She imagines a Scrabble game with Philippe. How often could she use the word *bon*?

And forget about words—she's lost the cultural clues! Is Philippe's shirt cool or dorky? It's kind of shiny—that wouldn't pass muster in New York. And he's got one earring that looks like a cross, but maybe it's an X. Does that mean something? Is he charming or creepy? Doesn't matter. She likes to look at him. He's handsome and that seems to translate well enough in any language.

He opens his book to a page that has a picture of a house. Pictures she likes. Pictures she can read. She feels like Cole, watching intently while Papa reads the text. If Philippe keeps this up for long, she'll need her blankie and a nap.

Philippe stops talking and points to a picture of a bedroom. He's pointed right at the bed! Yes, she wants to say: Let's go!

But she says, *"lit."* Amazing. When it matters, the words come to her. The important words.

"Le lit," Philippe says.

Who the hell cares? Feminine, masculine. When will the gender revolution come to France? Maybe it's a cross-dressing bed. Riley looks up. Philippe's watching her. Why does she have this goofy grin on her face because she's looking at a bed? Well, no fucking chance she can explain this one.

"Où est le lit?" she asks.

"Dans la chambre," Philippe says.

"Où est la chambre?" she asks.

He looks at her. Is he so pleased because they're having an infantile conversation or because they're talking about sex?

No one's talking about sex, Riley reminds herself. It's just in the air, wafting toward her.

"Dans la maison," Philippe says.

"Where is your *maison?"* Riley asks.

"En français," Philippe says.

"I know it's in France. Where in France?"

He shakes his head. But he's still smiling. He's left a couple of buttons open on his shiny shirt. Riley can see that he has a boy's chest, hairless and lean.

She has never cheated on Vic. She once desired a man who worked in the art department at her PR firm and she told Vic, and Vic told her he desired a woman who worked in the finance department of his company and that was the end of that. Tit for tat. Well, she hoped there wasn't any tit involved. There certainly wasn't any tat for her.

Is Vic cheating on her now? Is he really meeting boring
French businessmen every hour of the day and night? She asked
him once—mid-dinner on a date night—and he said, "My God,
Riley. Can't we even spend one night out without your ruin-
ing it?"

She had a sudden image of herself as a shrew, the kind of
woman a husband complained about to his office mates. Wasn't
she the siren a few years ago, the woman Vic boasted about?
"My wife loves sex," he once told a friend of theirs. "You lucky
fuck," the friend said. Whenever they finished making love,
Riley would whisper in Vic's ear: "You lucky fuck." And he
would fall asleep with a smile on his face.

She hasn't seen that smile in a long time.

"J'habite près du Centre Beaubourg," Philippe says.

She understood him! The Pompidou Center! But they call
it whatever he said. She remembers standing on the top floor
of the museum and looking out at the rooftops of Paris and
thinking: Everyone else is having a wonderful life. Just look.
Charming attic apartments, sex in a single bed, the smell of
bouillabaisse and hashish floating through the air.

Now she knows: Philippe is one of those people.

I had a wonderful life, she wants to say. She remembers the
bon voyage party her friends threw for them a few weeks before
they moved to Paris. She and Vic wore matching berets and
striped shirts (hers stretched over a pregnant belly). Mid-party
they had a fencing match with baguettes as weapons. They were
grown-up kids embarking on a grand adventure. "Will you
be lonely over there?" one friend asked her. "Not with Vic and
Cole and little Miss Wiggle Worm. Besides, it's Paris," she said.

Wonderful slips away, day by day. Why, even yesterday she
was more wonderful than today. Yesterday her mother didn't

have cancer. Riley has lost her mind in a tangle of thoughts and Philippe has asked a question.

She smiles.

He repeats it.

She shakes her head. *"No comprendo."*

"Je ne comprends pas," he corrects her.

Why bother trying to explain it's an expression in English— well, not in English exactly, but something everyone says in English even though it's in Spanish.

"Right," she says. "What you said."

Vic speaks French. He speaks it so well that he's now changed his name to Victor. He says that the French don't use nicknames and so he's now Victor. "The Victor." That's what she calls him when she's really annoyed, as in: "Will you be home for dinner, The Victor?" To which he usually responds no. He used to say "Don't call me that." But now he doesn't bother. "No" takes care of everything—it's an all-purpose word. In fact, it's the same word in French even if they do put an extra unnecessary letter on the end. *Non!* I won't be home for dinner!

But Riley is Riley in any language. "What am I supposed to call myself now," she asked The Victor. "AllRiledUp?"

"Clever," he said.

Of course he calls Gabi Gabrielle, which is her real name, but damned if Riley's going to start burdening her daughter with a name that's longer than she is. Cole is Cole is Cole is Cole. Thank God.

Does anyone call Philippe Phil? In bed, maybe? A kiss here, my Philistine? Sometimes sex draws a thing out, doesn't it?

So they're back to the *lit* and the *lampe* and all things *de la chambre*. Riley learns a few new words while gazing at the book. Then she imagines her mother in the bed in the picture. When

Riley was little she would climb in bed with her mother and
they would read, side by side, their cottony arms rubbing up
next to each other. Her mother often hummed, but she said she
didn't. And now Riley hums while she gives Cole a bath. It's the
same tune. How can she ask her mother what the tune is when
her mother says she never hums? Riley feels a kind of urgency
and peers at her mother in the bed. The image begins to fade
until *poof*—she's gone—and a goddamn tear splashes on the
page.

Philippe says something, real alarm on his lovely face, and
Riley wipes her eyes, shakes her head and says, *"Rien, rien."*
Amazing what words appear when she needs them.

But in a quick moment, Philippe is packing up. Men and
tears. She half expects him to dash out and leave her behind, but
at the last minute he gestures for her to follow him.

Whatever.

They stand outside the café, in the middle of the Marais,
looking at each other.

Philippe says something.

Riley smiles.

"Bon," he says.

He takes her arm and they start walking down rue des
Francs-Bourgeois.

For the first time in a year, Riley feels French. She's walking
next to a Frenchman—a handsome Frenchman at that—and instead of doctor's appointments and playground visits and *pain
au chocolat* shopping, there is only this: mystery. She has no idea
where they're going. She's been dropped from her life into a
French novel.

Never mind that Riley looks pathetically American. Before
she moved to Paris, everyone told her "Whatever you do, don't

wear sneakers." She left them all behind. And now, in a swift
change of fashion trends, every goddamn Frenchwoman is wearing little white sneakers. But it's not the clothes, it's the breasts.
No one in France has breasts this size. She tried buying a new
bra and got tired of the way the saleswomen rolled their eyes
and sadly shook their heads. And then there's the hair! She has
long, curly hair, messy hair, hair that won't be contained in rubber bands or hair clips. It explodes from her head like confetti.
"Cut it," Vic said. *"Non!"* she told him. She loves her hair.

So somehow she has arrived at a point in her life that she
looks like a porn star. She has big hair and high heels and enormous breasts. In New York, everyone would know that she's not
a porn star, because she's smart and funny and the clothes she
wears are sophisticated and she has her sneakers. But here,
there's only one way to translate this: "Fuck me!"

Maybe that's what Philippe plans, Riley thinks. She tucks
thoughts of her mother away—no, Mom, you're not coming
along for this ride!—and clicks her heels as she struggles to keep
up with Philippe's long stride.

The sky darkens as suddenly as a full eclipse of the sun and
then, in a flash of lightning and thunder, as if God is screaming,
Get sex out of your mind right now!, the heavens open up.
Philippe's grip tightens on Riley's arm and he leads her under
the canopy of a corner restaurant. In a second, a crowd of people huddle under this teeny canvas, and they are squeezed together.

The crowd oohs and aahs as if God were a fucking superstar.
Riley can barely see the street anymore—they're sandwiched
between so many people. Someone smells as if they had garlic
oatmeal for breakfast; someone else has the hiccups and the
whole crowd seems to jerk with each gasp of breath. Riley feels

her heartbeat racing—she's not sure if it's the drama of the heavens or Philippe's arm pressed into her breast. And for once, she doesn't have to speak. She gets this: it's weather and it's wild. No need for a running commentary. Just take it in.

Riley remembers a camping trip with Vic in Vermont— pre-kids, pre-marriage—when a storm woke them in the middle of the night, pounding their tent so loudly that they knew it was hail, a freak midsummer hailstorm, and Riley began to tremble, suddenly sure that the thin fabric would give way and they'd be iced to death. Vic climbed on top of her and in a quick moment their sleeping bags were unzipped, their clothes pulled off, and their bodies pounded each other in the most violent, urgent, ragged sex they ever had. Afterward, the hailstorm too had ended and they lay there, gasping, staring at the roof of the tent in the dark, side by side, their hands clasped together. They never spoke about it afterward, as if there were something shameful about the way they tore at each other. Riley wonders now: What would it take to bring Vic back to me?

A clap of thunder and Riley transports herself on a transatlantic journey from Vermont to Paris, from Vic to the French tutor, from the smell of pine trees to the smell of wet wool. The rain stops as abruptly as it started. The sky lightens. The crowd doesn't move as if they're not ready for the show to end. No one says a word. Riley almost expects a call: "Encore!" But eventually the first few people break away from their tight little gathering, and then the next, and then Philippe's arm leaves her breast. She sags a little—not her breast, which is firmly ensconced in an American 34 DD bra with underwire and wide straps—but her whole body feels a little post-orgasmic. The show is over.

Philippe looks at her. She feels closer to him now, as if they have shared something. And to her delight, he doesn't speak. He wraps that wonderful hand around her upper arm and leads her onward.

The sidewalks are crowded with people, everyone on the move again, and the city streets glisten with light reflecting off the puddles. Riley thinks of Cole and his new green rubber boots with the frog eyes on the tips—he should be splashing his way to the Place des Vosges instead of sitting in front of the TV with Fadwa or Fatah or Fadul's mother. Bad Mama! And tonight, when he wants Daddy to put him to bed, she'll have to explain: *It's you and me, babe.*

But no time for children! I'm off on a Parisian adventure! It's all about me-me-me!

How odd that a person can lose herself in a city, in a family, in a marriage. How odd that she never felt lonely when she lived alone all those years in New York, and now, wrapped in the tidy package of nuclear family, a member of every fucking expat group that exists in Paris, every moms' group for English-speakers, every wives' group for expats, she feels like she's the kid standing outside the school and everyone's gone home and her mother has forgotten to pick her up.

Do they call it nuclear because it's bound to explode?

She has not mentioned to her mother that her husband has gone AWOL on their marriage, that he's rarely home, that he barely touches her, that the last time she told a funny story about the crazy woman who yelled at her for breast-feeding in the park he said, "Maybe you shouldn't be breast-feeding any-more." When Riley found out that her pet name for Vic, "coo-coo," is something French people say to their infants, he told her, "Maybe you shouldn't call me that anymore." She has not mentioned to her mother that she wakes in the middle of the night with something like terror lodged in her chest. No wonder her mother forgot to metaphorically pick her up—she's a fraud and her mother knows it. She used to tell her mother everything and now she has spent a year telling her mother not to visit her in Paris, and now her mother has cancer.

"*Comment?*" Philippe asks.

She looks up at him. Has she said something? In what language? The language of grief?

"*Rien,*" she assures him. "My mother hums when she's thinking and apparently I do that, too."

"*En français,*" Philippe says.

"Oh, shut the fuck up," she tells him.

He laughs. *Fuck*—the international language.

He slides his hand on her lower back as he presses her in front of him. The crowd is so thick on the sidewalk that they can't walk side by side and he keeps his hand there, guiding her forward, like a dancer, leading her through complicated moves on the dance floor. She is a terrible dancer; she doesn't know how to follow a guy, or maybe she's never been with a guy who knows how to lead. Before their wedding she and Vic took a couple of dance lessons and they were dismal failures, bumping into each other, turning the wrong way, smacking into each other's shoes. One night they got stoned and danced in the empty living room of their new apartment and suddenly they could do it—they were Fred and Ginger—they spun and dipped and swooned. A week later, at their own wedding, they had to bear-hug through the first dance, too embarrassed to fumble through a merengue in front of the crowd. "I can't feel your lead," Riley had whispered to Vic. "What do you want, a steamroller?" Vic asked. "Steamroll me, baby," Riley whispered in his ear when they made love that night.

Philippe's hand slides around her waist and pulls her to a stop.

"Nous sommes arrivés," he announces.

She looks around. They're in the middle of the block; all around them people walk in every direction and cars blast their horns. She looks at Philippe, who's gazing up—at a building that might have been built in the fifties and hasn't been washed since. It would look like just about any building except it's in the middle of Paris and every other building is a piece of art. This is not. It's got a flat surface that is dull and soot-covered, the windows grimy and dark. Who lives here?

Apparently her dashing French tutor lives in this dump, because he's tapping in a code and opening the front door. Riley's feet are frozen in place. She hears a chorus of voices—Vic, her mom, Cole, Gabi—all shouting at her. She's being stoned by words.

"Riley," Philippe says, and the voices vanish, her feet thaw, and she's hurrying inside the door. She was never a pushover before—now the sound of her name in this man's mouth turns her into a hussy.

The elevator smells of dirty diapers. It's hard to think about sex, and Riley tries not to breathe, as if she'd be allowing Gabi to enter her mind if she thought about dirty diapers. How does she know the babysitter's mother will change Gabi's diaper? She once left Gabi with her mother on her last visit home, six months ago, and came back from the beach with Cole to find Gabi drenched and soiled. "I thought they made diapers stronger these days," her mother said, unbothered by the mess.

"Next time, you take care of the baby and I'll go to the beach with the munchkin." Riley's mom prefers Cole to Gabi, and has never tried to hide it.

So the not breathing on the elevator didn't work. She's got Gabi and Cole and her mother all living in her head now. *Go away,* she wants to scream. *There's no room for you in this bed!*

The bed turns out to be a futon, and an unmade one at that. Philippe throws open the door to his apartment and Riley sees immediately that she has made a terrible mistake. There is nothing romantic about a loser. And Philippe must be a loser—who else could live like this? There's the pea-green futon, the beer cans (why would anyone drink beer in the land of Burgundy and Bordeaux?) strewn all over the floor, the poster of Angelina Jolie, the guitar in the middle of the floor. At least that's a sign of culture. The guy must strum on his guitar, then drop it like a sack of potatoes.

Philippe tosses his jacket on the floor and walks into the kitchen. Riley stands there, waiting to flee. It's easy, she thinks. Turn around, walk out the door. Send a check to the language school. Never see this man again.

But he returns, carrying two glasses of champagne.

She takes a glass and sips. It's flat and warm but it tastes wonderful. She sips some more.

When she looks up at Philippe he leans over and kisses her, a long kiss that seems to include the exchange of champagne from his mouth into hers. It's creepy and she almost chokes, but then his hand reaches under her shirt and touches her skin. She hasn't been touched in a long time. Her mind goes silent, and her body goes liquid.

He picks her up and carries her to the bed. They tumble down—did he trip on a beer can or did she suddenly get too heavy for him?—and they fall in a tangle of limbs on the thin futon. Riley bangs her elbow hard, but Philippe's kissing her neck and the pain gets lost in the heat coursing through her body. She tears at his clothes, pulling them off. He gets stuck on one of her buttons and she pushes him back, then yanks the shirt off her. He makes a deep animal sound at the sight of her breasts and dives in.

Philippe slides his hand into her panties and she whimpers.

Riley bites his neck and he groans.

Philippe's finger slips inside her—she's already wet despite months of thinking she'd gone frigid sometime after Gabi's birth—and Riley gasps.

Riley's hand grabs his cock—when did his pants come off? What's on the end of his cock?—and he moans.

Philippe's finger presses deep inside her, his mouth pulls at her breast, his cock grows in her hand. Riley's panting but that's the sound of his heavy breath in her ear and the noise makes her wrap her legs around him, pull him inside her, then pull him out. "Condom," she says.

"*Quoi?*"

"Whatever," she says. "Just put one on."

Philippe reaches for the side of the futon and of course he has a bowlful of condoms or whatever they're called here, and in a flash his lovely penis—yes, it's uncircumcised and it's a thing of beauty—is swathed in latex and it towers above her, pointing every which way in its wonderful excitement, until it finds its way home.

Both of them sigh—deep, long, luxurious sighs.

And then they begin to move together and the song in Riley's head, the song she's been humming since childhood, spills out of her, a nursery rhyme, a Russian folk song, something her grandmother taught her mother, something her mother hummed to her while bathing her and dressing her and walking her to school, and while Philippe batters her with his cock, bites her breasts, pulls at her hair, Riley cries. It's a flood up there, tears spilling down the side of her face, and Philippe washes her face with his tongue, a tongue as wondrous as his penis.

He doesn't stop. He's grunting, making some kind of *whoo-whoo-whoo* sound. His body is hard, his muscles taut, his movements powerful. Riley watches him, amazed—it's a feat of athleticism, this kind of sex, it's a descent into darkness, it's a wild-animal mating ritual.

When he comes, he hoots—a cowboy shout, a rodeo ride, this bucking bronco—and then he collapses on top of her, their bodies slick with each other's sweat.

So. This is sex.

Every other sex she has experienced in her life had something to do with love, or the search for love, or the end of love. This is just sex.

Her mind floods with words again.

Amazing. For however many minutes that took, Riley had turned off her brain. And now it's someplace new. She's thinking about love.

Not love for Philippe—no! How soon till she can shower, dress, and flee! Not love for The Victor—no! Love is lost, she's sure of that now. Love cannot be found, no matter how hard one looks in all the nooks and crannies of their foolish, over-furnished apartment. Not love for all the old boyfriends who didn't know how to have sex like this—Franklin and his too-small penis, Luca and his wham-bam-thank-you-ma'am performance, Terry and his doughboy body, Johnny and his stick-it-in-during-the-middle-of-the-night obsession, Jesse and his terror of the female netherlands.

She's thinking about her love for Paris!

Paris. The city of sex. The city of clandestine affairs. The city of handsome French tutors in pathetic apartments. The city where the *pain au chocolat* you eat in the morning is only the first erotic taste of the day. The city where you can stop talking long enough to hear the song your mother sang.

Just in time—just as Riley remembers her mother's phone call this morning—Philippe turns her over, holds her hands spread open on the bed, pushes her legs apart with his knees, and enters her from behind.

We are speaking the same language, she thinks.

And this time the sex is even harder—he bites her shoulder at one point, he pushes so hard inside her that she feels herself opening, breaking up, crumbling, splitting.

When he comes, he falls beside her on the bed.

She puts her hand between her legs and makes herself come. She's almost there, and he's not going to do anything about it. He watches, his face full of something like wonder.

When she's done, she's crying again. This time the tears are for Vic, the old Vic, the old marriage, the love vanished in thin Parisian air. Riley slides away from Philippe and hobbles to the shower. Sure enough, it's a pit, a hole, and she doesn't mind one bit. She washes and cries and washes some more. She hums.

Philippe is sleeping when she comes out. She finds her clothes and gets dressed. A button has torn off her shirt—it gapes open, exposing her baby belly. Who cares? She's a sexpot.

She leaves, pulling the door closed behind her. She doesn't want to talk to him. Besides, she doesn't speak the language.

•••

On the way home Riley sees a couple walking down the street, their pigtailed little girl between them, all of them holding hands. To let Riley pass, the dad drops the girl's hand, like the child's game London Bridge Is Falling Down. Riley walks past and then looks behind her—sure enough, the little girl skips ahead, untethered, and the parents walk with a gap between them.

Riley imagines that anything that once held Vic and her together—love, passion, Cole's hands—has fallen down. She knows that cheating on Vic didn't kill love. Love was already gasping its last dying breath. Even if Vic has been cheating on her, it's what he did to fill the space between them.

She race-walks down the street, her heels clattering on the pavement.

Twenty minutes later, she is home. Gabi is taking her nap—with a clean diaper—and Cole is playing checkers with the babysitter's mom. Riley pays the woman twice what she'd normally pay and bows too many times, backing the woman out the door. Cole wraps his arms around Riley's leg as if she's been gone for years.

"Let's call Nana," Riley says.

"Nana!" Cole repeats, rapturously. He loves his grandma.

It is early morning in Florida—her mother will be reading the paper in the sunroom overlooking the golf course. It is early afternoon in Paris—Riley and Cole sit in the breakfast nook overlooking the courtyard below. A little girl, the concierge's granddaughter, stands in the middle of the courtyard, her mouth open in a wide O.

"Open the window," Riley says. "I think she's singing."

Cole climbs over the chair and slides the window open. It squeaks and the girl looks up at them, caught mid-note. She pauses and the sound of *tey-tey-tey* hangs in the air. In a quick moment, she's singing again, in a thin, high voice. It's a beautiful song and she watches them while she sings.

"Mom," Riley says when her mother answers the phone.

"Don't start calling me every two minutes, Miss Worrywart," her mom says.

"I just want to talk to you," Riley says quietly.

"Is my favorite little man there?"

"Cole," Riley says, handing him the phone. "She wants you."

"Nana?" Cole says.

He listens, but he never once takes his eyes off the girl in the courtyard below. He has his grandmother's voice in one ear and a child's song in the other ear. His smile spreads across his face.

"I love you, too," he says, probably to both of them.

He hands Riley the phone.

"I'm fine," her mother says right away. "I'll have the surgery, they'll take it out."

"Chemo," Riley says. That's all she can say.

"So I'll do chemo. I won't be the first person in the world."

"What does the doctor say?"

"He says we should all be so tough at sixty-four years old. He says what I already know. I'm a fighter."

"How come you didn't give any of that fight to me?"

"You got plenty of fight. Who else goes to live on the other side of the world with two babies?"

Riley looks around the kitchen—it's all white, as if aliens or nuns live here.

"You're the only one I ever talk to."

"You don't talk to your husband?"

"No, Ma. Not much."

"He's never there. Who takes his bride to the other side of the world and leaves her all alone?"

"Vic."

"Oh, baby."

Luckily Cole is staring out the window so he doesn't see the tears pouring down Riley's face.

"I'm coming home," Riley says.

"No. Stay where you are and fix your problems. You have two babies. You can't just go gallivanting across the world every time you have a little fight with your husband."

"It's not a little fight. And it's not across the world. It's an ocean. It's a six-hour flight." Riley's mother never left the United States, never jumped on a plane at a moment's notice, never served a cheese course after dinner.

"Tell Mr. International Businessman to pay a little attention to his wife. Tell him his mother-in-law said so."

"It's not so easy, Ma."

"Nothing's easy, Riley. No one ever said life is easy. You kids—"

"Don't start that." Riley hates the "you kids" lecture. No one ever served her her life on a silver platter anyway.

Her mother is quiet again, and it begins to worry Riley. Her mother has never waited for words to come to her. They just spill from her mouth.

"Your father came home to eat dinner with his family every night of the week," her mother finally says.

Riley has heard this chant for years, and though she knows it's not true—he worked late and she usually ate dinner hours before he came home—she loves the memory of her father's entrance each evening. At the front door, he'd take off his suit jacket and place it over Riley's shoulders. He'd perch his hat on her head. She'd smell his aftershave, his sweat, the stuffy air of his accounting office, and she'd feel the weight of him as the jacket pulled on her small shoulders.

"I miss Dad," Riley says. It's not something she ever says to her mother. She remembers the years of her mother's grief after her father died ten years ago, years when she worried that her mother would suddenly grow old. But then her mother moved to Florida and forged a new life for herself—grief was no match for her. Riley's own sense of loss became quiet, hidden, as if now, as an adult, she doesn't have a right to miss her daddy the way she does.

"I miss him, too," her mother says. "It's quiet in an apartment all by yourself. I leave the TV on all day just for the noise."

"Who's taking you for your surgery?" Riley asks.

She has no idea if her mom has boyfriends, though she seems to have a lot of men in her life. There's Art, the trainer at the gym who might be gay, but if he isn't, go get him, Mom! And Stitch, the construction worker who has dinner over a few times a week, even though there isn't any more work to do at the condo. Last Riley heard, a guy named Al was swimming laps with Mom every morning.

"Wally," Mom finally says.

"Who's Wally?"

"You know about Wally."

"Never heard his name."

"Doesn't matter. He's just driving me to the hospital. I'll be fine."

"What doesn't matter?"

"Who he is. He's just a ride."

"Does he know he's just a ride?"

Philippe is just a ride, she thinks. Why didn't I listen to my mother years ago?

"Go take your prince to one of those fancy bakeries. Tell him Nana wants to buy him one of those French pastries you keep talking about."

Riley nods and mumbles something and hangs up the phone. Cole is still spellbound by the chanteuse below. Riley looks out the window.

The girl in the courtyard finishes her song and takes a bow. She blows a kiss and Cole catches it, a trick Nana had taught him six months ago. He is in love, Riley thinks. For the rest of his life, this will be love.

"Nana wants to buy you a *pain au chocolat*," Riley says.

"How? Nana in Florida."

"She told me to buy you one. When Gabi wakes up, we'll go for a walk, sweetie."

"Mama cry," Cole says, looking at her for the first time.

"Runny nose," Riley says. "Gotta catch it." And she heads for the Kleenex box on the kitchen counter.

With Gabi in her Snugli and Cole by her side, Riley decides to embark on a quest: to eat the best damn *pain au chocolat* in all of Paris. At the last expat moms' group—another miserable experience—everyone swapped favorite parks, favorite children's clothing stores, favorite child-friendly restaurants, favorite pediatricians, and of course, favorite pâtisseries. Next meeting, Riley imagines herself spreading the word: Best tutor for a midday fuck fest—Philippe!

She heads toward *numéro uno* on the pâtisserie list. It has stopped raining and she needs to shake the spooks from her psyche. Somehow between now and late tonight when The Victor crawls into bed, she's got to figure out what to do with her life.

Her cell phone rings.

"Hello?"

"Riley."

"Philippe?" His voice sounds different, as if it's been dipped in honey.

"Meet me for a glass of wine."

"You're speaking English."

"The French lesson is over."

"You speak English. All this time you speak English."

"Not so well. But your French is—how you say—it sucks."

His accent is not Maurice Chevalier charming but kind of high and whiny. He's not sexy in English. In fact, he's Philip in English. She would never fuck a Philip.

"I've got the kids, Philippe. Real life and all of that."

"Oh."

She thinks of his uncircumcised penis waving in the air above her. She almost runs into a street light but Cole shouts, *"Maman!"* Weird. On the street Cole calls her *Maman*. In their apartment he calls her Mama. How does a two-year-old navigate such complicated terrain?

"Sorry, baby."

"No need to be sorry," Philippe says.

"I was—"

"Bring the children. They are filming on the quai. Some famous American actress is here. We can watch, all of us together."

One quick fuck—all right, two—and he's creating a new nuclear family, Riley thinks. Let's blow that one up before it even hits Code Orange.

"Listen, Philippe—"

"*T'es belle. T'es magnifique, chérie.*"

"Okay," Riley says. She shakes her head. In some distant country her old friends scream at her: *Pathetic fool!* "Where?" she asks.

He gives her an address and whispers something in French. In a quick moment, he is her sexy lover again.

But she doesn't want a sexy lover! She just wants someone to walk next to her in Paris, someone taller than three feet.

She leads the kids toward the nearest métro, already scrambling in her brain for a way out of this mess.

Cole used to love the métro, used to pull Riley toward the swirly green gables beckoning them to the underworld of speedy trains and flashy billboards. He watched the people who moved from car to car, making speeches, playing guitar, juggling balls, a wacked-out subterranean circus.

"What he say, *Maman?*" he'd ask when the homeless man would stand at the front of the car and recite some story to the captive audience.

"I don't know," she'd tell him honestly.

Then, as his French got better, he understood their terrible stories: *Ladies and gentlemen. My wife has a broken leg. There is no heat in our apartment. My oldest children are sick from the cold, the youngest one has a rare disease. I can no longer work because my child is at the hospital.* Cole would bury his face in Riley's coat, hiding his tears, worried that the child in the hospital would die and the man would never get work and the poor *maman* could not walk. "We'll give the man money," Riley would say, as if one euro would solve the problems of the world.

"We have to take the métro," Riley tells Cole now, urging him down into the underworld of misery and hardship. *We have to go see my lover*, she won't say, but she presses her hand on his small back and he's such a good boy that he heads dutifully down-down-down the stairs and toward her own personal Satan.

Thankfully there are no speeches on the métro today, just a boy doing some kind of break dancing—though Riley thinks they call it something else now. Already she's too old for the latest fads. Cole applauds when the boy is done, and Riley fishes out a euro for Cole to put in the boy's filthy palm.

Gabi pokes her head out of the Snugli, watching the world. She's a quiet baby and Riley loves her for it. She loves the weight of the baby pressed against her chest, the smell of her powdery scalp, the tufts of strawberry-blond hair that swirl on her head like a halo.

They climb the stairs from the métro and for a moment they're blinded—it has stopped raining again, and the brilliant sun reflects from all the puddles that have gathered in the street. Riley finds her movie-star sunglasses and hides behind them. In Paris the women wear small, dignified glasses, arty things with frames of red, purple, bronze. She won't give up her oversize tortoise-framed specs. They make her feel like Gwyneth dashing over to Paris for a little shopping expedition.

She pulls out her *plan*, the little blue book of maps that she carries like a Bible, and finds the First Arrondissement—then rue de Rivoli, where Philippe awaits. She has never arrived anywhere in Paris without getting lost. The streets are treacherous, evil places that might deliver you to a canal instead of a street corner. She will not ask directions—it's useless, all that finger-pointing and hand-waving and word-flying.

But miraculously, the entrance to the courtyard of the Louvre is across the street, and in front of it is Philippe.

He waits for her to cross the street, then he steps toward her and leans forward to kiss her.

She pulls back.

"*Les enfants,*" she says.

"Aha. So now you speak French," he says.

He shakes her hand. That is what they do when he comes to her apartment for her French lessons. And he shakes Cole's hand and says, "*Bonjour, monsieur.*"

"*Bonjour, monsieur,*" Cole repeats, his accent perfect.

Philippe leans forward to kiss the top of Gabi's head, and while he does it he sneaks a hand onto Riley's neck. Both Gabi and Riley make some kind of whimpering sound.

"*Arrête,*" Riley says.

"Your French is very good, *madame.*"

"It's the only damn word you learn here in the playgrounds. *Arrête, Antoine. Arrête, Marie-Hélène. Arrête. Arrête.*"

"You are spending time in the wrong playground," Philippe says. "Follow me."

He leads them into a passageway with windowed sides that show displays of ancient art—sculptures and relics, half-excavated buildings. Riley glances to each side as they hurry by. She still has not visited the Louvre. In fact, in a year of living in Paris, she has missed most of the tourist spots. That's not where you go with two babies in Paris. These are adult playgrounds; again the day feels foreign and thrilling to her.

They enter the courtyard of the Louvre, and even though Riley has walked through here once, with Victor on a Sunday morning, both babies in strollers, she remembers only their argument about an office party that didn't allow spouses.

"Why not?" she had asked.

"The French keep their private lives and public lives separate," Vic told her.

"Why?" she asked. She felt like Cole—*why-why-why?*

"Maybe the wife shouldn't meet the pretty assistant," Vic said.

"Whose wife? Whose pretty assistant?"

"Theoretically."

"That's absurd. That's crazy," Riley insisted. "That's so—so blind."

"Blind is good," Vic said.

"You think everything they do is good," Riley argued.

"Sometimes we have to see the world through different glasses," Vic explained calmly, as if talking to a two-and-a-half-year-old.

Riley has found a new pair of glasses.

Now she's awed by the daring of I. M. Pei's modern glass pyramid in the center of these lovely, ancient buildings. She looks around, eyes wide open. She hears a storm of language—French, English, Spanish, German, Arabic—and turns her head in each direction. Everyone comes from a different country, everyone speaks a different language, everyone gathers to look at this. History. Art. Grace.

"There is a café here," Philippe tells her, leading them to one side of the courtyard.

"Do we have time before the filming?"

"I think so," Philippe says. "We will sit for a moment and I will buy you a drink."

They enter the arcade of the Louvre. Café Marly fills the vaulted space with lush red decor, gold and teal tones. It's stunning and glamorous and it's crowded with well-dressed people.

No babies here, no wild two-year-olds, no breast-leaking moms. Riley looks at Philippe with a worried expression.

"We will not stay for very long," Philippe says.

"*Maman,*" Cole says, pointing to the group of children playing with a ball in front of the fountain.

"Go ahead," Riley says. "I'll watch you from the café."

Cole dashes off, his arms turning into airplane wings.

Philippe and Riley are seated at a small table with a perfect view of the courtyard and the pyramid. Riley keeps Gabi in her Snugli and pats the baby's head as if to reassure her that *Maman* can have a glass of wine with her French lover at this fabulous café in the center of grand Paris.

"This *pain au chocolat* comes from the best pâtisserie in all of Paris," Riley says, digging into her backpack and producing a somewhat squished bag.

"*J'aime pas,*" Philippe tells her.

"What?"

"I can't eat chocolate."

"That's impossible."

He makes that peculiar French face—raised eyebrows, puffed lips—that seems to mean all things: *Who cares? What do you know? I think you're grand.*

Riley takes a bite of her pastry. It is perfect but so is every other *pain au chocolat* she eats.

"I wanted to look at you," Philippe says. He's looking at her, all right. Did she forget to get dressed when she ran out the door? Is there not a baby perched right there on her mountainous chest?

"So who's the actress?" she asks.

"Dana Hurley. She is making a movie with the great director Pascale Duclaux."

"Dana Hurley's the real deal," Riley says. "I'd love to see her."

Philippe is staring at her, his mouth slightly parted.

"Where are they filming?" Riley asks, glancing in the courtyard at Cole, who swings his leg out to kick the ball, misses completely, and falls back on his butt with a hoot of laughter.

"On the Pont des Arts. Soon. We will have a glass of wine first."

"I thought you drink beer."

He looks confused. "Oh, the apartment. I am sorry. I did not know—"

"Wine is good," she says quickly. "Let's have wine."

They order two glasses. Riley looks around. The café is crowded, of course, and all the tables seem to be filled with couples. One young couple has locked lips and, for a bewildering moment, Riley thinks the woman looks like a very young version of herself; the guy could be Vic before he grew up and became The Victor. Did we ever paw each other in public? she thinks. Never.

She remembers one time she kissed Vic in front of his parents the first weekend she met them in Ohio.

"My parents aren't really comfortable with that kind of thing," he had whispered, taking her hand so as not to upset her. They were sitting on the couch, mid–Super Bowl party.

"What kind of thing?" she whispered back.

"Sex."

"That was a kiss. You want sex, I'll show you sex."

"Later," he promised. He asked his father to turn up the volume on the TV so they could all hear the football announcers instead of his crazy girlfriend.

Philippe leans toward her across the table.

"*Ce soir*," he murmurs.

"*Ce soir* I'm making macaroni and cheese."

"Feed me," he whispers.

"Five's a crowd at the dinner table," she says, though there will only be three of them, of course. She points at the baby— as if Gabi could possibly understand this conversation—but Philippe either ignores her or she's not using the international symbol for "Shut the hell up." She remembers her father often saying "Not in front of the children," which meant to her: *Pay attention! Parental drama ahead!*

"I want to see you again," Philippe says.

Riley spreads her arms wide—*lookee here*. But what's here is a baby girl staring back at him. Girls are so damned intuitive— maybe she knows what's going on. Who needs words when a guy has sex written all over his face?

"Let's talk about your life," Riley says, patting Gabi's head. She spends so much time patting the baby's head that she's surprised the kid has any hair at all. Maybe that's why the stuff whirls around her head like it's hula dancing.

"*Bof*," Philippe says.

"Okay. Translate that. I've been here a year and every damn person I meet says *bof* in every conversation. *Bof. Bof. Bof.* What's up with the *bof*?"

"There is no translation," Philippe says.

"What kind of tutor are you?"

"The best kind," he says, smiling his Satan smile. The shirt is definitely not cool. It is shiny-smarmy, not shiny-hip. I'm learning, Riley thinks. I may not know words, but I know my shirts.

"So. You got a girlfriend?" she asks. There was no sign of a female touch in that lovely abode she visited earlier, but who knows? The girl could be a beer hog.

"Elle s'appelle Riley," Philippe says.

"Got that wrong," she tells him.

"Pourquoi pas?"

"Parce que I've got this load of love in my lap and the other running in circles over there."

"It is not the same kind of love."

"We're talking love?"

"We do not need to talk. We need to love."

"You're talking about s-e-x."

"Faire l'amour. To make love."

"In our country—"

"You are not in your country."

"And in your country love and s-e-x are the same thing?"

"Perhaps."

"Un-fucking-believable. I love this city."

"C'est vrai?"

"Today. Right now. This second. I heart Paris."

With that the waiter pours their wine and they clink glasses.

The sky darkens; thick black clouds have moved in again. Riley puts her monster shades up on her head.

"I used to think that every time I had s-e-x I loved the guy," she tells Philippe. "Now I know. It's s-e-x that I love."

"But it is the man. It is always the man."

"What's always the man?"

"You have loved him. You have loved me."

"Sorry, Charlie."

Philippe looks confused.

"It's an expression. I know your name."

"Bon." Philippe looks unhappy, as if she called him the wrong name in the heat of passion.

"I think you're wrong," Riley says. "You're just a ride."

"*Je ne comprends pas.*"

"You made me feel good today. Thanks. But it ain't love."

"We need each other. All of us. We cannot be alone."

Riley looks around. Philippe must be talking some kind of Parisian truth, at least in this café. Not a solitary soul in sight. The make-out couple looks ready to tear up some bedsheets.

"Anyway, *c'est fini.* I'm not heading your way tomorrow for an afternoon delight. If you know what I mean."

"*Pourquoi pas?* A few hours ago you were very, how you say, with passion."

"But I'm not with passion now. I'm with kids now."

The littler of those kids starts to squirm in her Snugli.

"I don't want to breast-feed her in the middle of the café," Riley mutters, fishing for a pacifier in her backpack.

"I will be very happy to see you breast-feed."

"Yeah, I bet."

"Americans believe in groups," Philippe says. "You have all your expat groups and your *maman* groups and your book club groups. Do your groups make you not lonely?"

Riley shakes her head. She is most acutely aware of how lonely she is every time she enters someone's apartment for one of her many group meetings and hears the clamor of so many voices and sees the spread of food and tries to find a place for herself in the middle of it all.

Riley tried to befriend someone at the last expat meeting. While most women boasted about their husbands' positions as CEO of World Bank or editor in chief of *Newsweek Europe* or head of Apple's international division, a shy bohemian woman introduced herself by saying, "I have to be here while my husband plays in Paris." Riley assumed the woman was mocking the guy. But no, he was the new lead violinist of the Paris Symphony Orchestra.

"Want to get together one day?" Riley had boldly asked the woman. "I don't know many people here."

"Sorry," she had said, "but I'm immersing myself in French life while I'm here."

Riley felt like a fifth-grade misfit. She wanted to kick the woman's shins. Instead, she wandered back to the smoked salmon canapés on the dining room table and drank a fast glass of cheap white wine.

"Here in Paris we believe in two people," Philippe says. "It is only two people who can *faire l'amour.*"

"Let's start walking," Riley says, standing quickly. "I want to settle the baby down."

She rocks the baby, standing in place. Philippe finishes his wine in a gulp and tosses some money on the table.

"Do not be angry," he says sweetly as they walk out to the courtyard.

"I'm not angry," Riley says. "I'm confused."

Cole leaves the group of kids and races to Riley's side. He looks up in her face.

"It's okay, *Maman,*" he says, taking her hand.

What goes on in that complicated little mind of his?

"I love you, sweetheart," Riley says. "Let's take a walk to the river, okay?"

"The river," Cole says happily. And off they go, the four of them. Sleep with a guy and *voilà!* You've got yourself a spanking new family. Would Vic notice if he slid between the sheets tonight and bumped up against Philippe? Again, that penis waves jubilantly in Riley's mind, and she shakes the image away.

"What happens if it rains when they're filming?" she asks.

"*On verra,*" he says.

She doesn't ask what that means. Whatever it is, it sounds better in French.

The crowd is enormous at the quai du Louvre. As far as Riley can see, people are lined up at the side of the promenade, staring out toward the river.

"I didn't know the French were starstruck like this," Riley says to Philippe. They're pressed together at the street corner, waiting for the light to change. Everyone seems to be headed for the same place, and when the light changes they shuffle along with the crowd.

"We love the cinema. We love art. We appreciate the work of our great directors."

"Face it, Philippe. You're all star-fuckers."

"I would fuck the star, yes."

"She's a middle-aged woman," Riley says.

"In our country, we love all women."

"Love, love, love. If the French do so much loving all the time, why is everyone so angry?"

Philippe leans over and kisses Riley, missing her lips and brushing against her cheek.

"*Arrête,*" Riley says. She looks at Cole, who is singing to himself, ignoring his mother and her tutor.

"*Je suis méchant,*" Philippe whispers.

Riley knows that expression—another common playground phrase. Bad boy. Man, is he ever.

They cross the street, step over the low fence that is supposed to keep pedestrians from walking on the grass but is apparently ignored by everyone at times of international crisis like filming in progress, and they gather with the hordes of people near the river.

She wiggles through the crowd—a hard thing to do with a baby on her double-D chest, Cole in front of her, Philippe behind her with a hand on her rump—and she finds an unpopulated patch of grass under a tree. Front-row seats.

"Bravo," Philippe says, and his hand slips away.

They all gaze out at the river. Across the way is the Left Bank, with its grand old apartment buildings, and to the right, the majestic Musée d'Orsay. Farther down, the Eiffel Tower peeks out above the rooftops. Riley's mouth hangs open. Paris. For a year she's been living somewhere else, somewhere dark and bleak. It's like she's just arrived, freshly fucked and wearing rose-colored glasses.

"Bed, *Maman*," Cole says.

Riley pulls her eyes away from the view across the river and gazes down at the pedestrian bridge. There's a bed in the middle of the bridge. In fact, it looks a little like it too has been freshly fucked. A tangle of sheets sprawl across the mattress.

"A bed?" she says.

Philippe mumbles a rush of words in French.

"*Expliquez* everything, *s'il vous plaît*," Riley insists.

"I don't know," Philippe says. "But I have the great hope to see Dana Hurley in that bed."

"Naked."

"*Bien sûr.*"

"In front of the children."

"It is art."

"It is weird."

"They're making a movie," Riley tells Cole. "They're going to film a scene and put it in a movie. It's not real."

No one says anything.

"That makes no sense," Riley tells herself aloud. "It's perfectly real. We're looking at it."

"*C'est vrai,*" Philippe says.

She puts her hand on Cole's head. He looks up at her, wide-eyed.

"You know how when someone dies in a movie, they don't really die? It's an actor pretending he's dead? So if someone does something in that bed, they're just pretending."

Cole keeps looking at her, waiting for something better. She hasn't got it.

"You explain it," she says to Philippe. She says the same thing to Vic often. When he comes home at the end of a long day, she'd like him to answer all the questions that Cole asks. Sometimes it is too hard for her to explain the simplest things: "Why Daddy have to work?" "Why Daddy go away?" "Why Mama cry?"

"*On verra,*" Philippe says.

So much for men and their explanations.

But Cole is happy with that, and he goes back to watching the bed.

There are a couple of tents at one end of the bridge and a swarm of people around the bed. Riley spots a director's chair and a red-haired woman perched in it. She's waving her hands and shouting.

"There's your great director," Riley says, pointing.

"*Mais oui,*" Philippe says, sighing, as if he has attained nirvana. He didn't sigh like that in bed, Riley thinks. He must save his sighs for art.

And then, in a blinding flash, the lights around the bed all illuminate and the bed itself becomes a kind of holy site, an oasis of white, a beckoning, a call. The crowd heaves a collective sigh—whatever the hell is going on out there, Riley is missing it. So it's a mattress on a bridge in the middle of the river. What's up with that?

Out of the absolute silence of the wondrous crowd comes a squeak, then a squall, then a bellow. Her baby is bawling.

"Shhhh," Riley says, patting Gabi's head.

Philippe shoots her dagger looks; even Cole looks up as if he's about to belt her for failing to observe this sacred ceremony without the proper decorum. Fuck decorum, Riley thinks. The kid is hungry.

She slides down along the trunk of the tree until she's sitting on its roots. She pulls Gabi from the Snugli and quickly unbuttons her blouse. She pulls her bra up and over her breasts and lets the baby latch on for dear life. *Ahhh.* Now Riley releases her own deep sigh. This is love.

While Gabi suckles and everyone else watches some stupid-ass scene on the bridge below—between Philippe's legs Riley can see a naked young woman writhing on the bed, a pompous ass circling the bed as if he's Elvis Presley incarnate—Riley thinks about love.

It's not s-e-x, though s-e-x is a grand substitute for love. It's this child, this breast, this flow of milk. It's Cole, watching his first naked woman in his life, only a short time after listening to the love song of a young girl in the courtyard below. It's her mother in Florida, who has asked her every day if she could come visit, knowing that Riley is unhappy even though Riley never said a word. And in that moment, Riley knows what she has to do. Love doesn't just sit around watching. Love jumps on a plane and shows up.

She takes out her cell phone. She clicks her mom's name and in moments her mother's voice is in her ear.

"That's three times in one day," her mom says.

"I'm coming home. I'm your ride. Don't argue," Riley says.

"I'm fine—"

"Listen," Riley says. "In a few months you'll come visit me in Paris. You'll love it here. I'll take you to the Eiffel Tower, we'll ride on a *bateau-mouche*. I haven't done any of those things. But right now, I'm coming to Florida."

"Why are you whispering?"

"Because everyone's watching some film being made. Dana Hurley is in it. Oh, I think I can see her. She's standing next to a bed on a bridge, and there's some bare-assed *chiquita* doing some sex-kitten act on the bed."

"Where's Cole?"

"Watching. It's art, Mom."

"I don't understand how you kids raise kids these days."

"Yeah, well."

"You can't come rushing home, Riley. You're married."

"I hate it."

"No, you don't."

"Not it. Him. Vic."

"Oh. Vic."

They're both quiet for a moment. Finally her mother says, "I thought so."

"I want something else. I don't know what."

Riley hears something whirring in the background.

"What's that noise?"

"I'm making a smoothie. It's an anti-cancer smoothie. Think it will work?"

"Yeah. We'll make it work."

"Thank you, sweetheart," her mom says, and she's crying,

making gulping sounds that blend with the whirring sounds so that it's an orchestral event on the other end.

Riley doesn't cry. She smiles and lets Gabi suckle and watches Cole gawk. This is love. She'll go home with her children and take care of her mother who won't let anyone in the world take care of her. Maybe she'll even let her mother take care of *her*.

Then there's a roar of thunder, a gasp from the crowd, and the skies open up. Cole steps back and the three of them—she, Gabi, and Cole—huddle together under the canopy of the tree while the rain soaks the bed, the actors, the crowd, Philippe, and Paris in all its glory.

Jeremy and Chantal

JL 08

PONT DES ARTS

rue de Rivoli

Quai des Grands Augustins

Voie Georges Pompidou

ÎLE DE LA CITÉ

NOTRE DAME

Boulevard Beaumarchais

Pont Saint-Louis

JARDIN BLEU

ÎLE SAINT-LOUIS

Boulevard Saint-Germain

Boulevard Henri IV

Quai de la Tournelle

rue Monge

Seine R

Quai Saint-Bernard

rue Mouffetard

GRANDE MOSQUÉE DE PARIS

JARDIN DES PLANTES

M

METRO CENSIER-DAUBENTON

GRANDE GALERIE DE L'EVOLUTION

Boulevard Raspail

Boulevard de Port-Royal

Boulevard Saint-Marcel

Boulevard Arago

*D*o I want to kiss my French tutor because I've had a fight with my wife, Jeremy thinks, or did I fight with my wife because I suddenly desire my French tutor?

It's his last day with Chantal, and all he can think of is his mouth on hers.

Every other day he thought of conjugations and obscure nouns and colloquial expressions. Now he thinks of the space exposed by her open blouse, that blush of skin, the heat he feels when his eyes dip into the hollow of her neck.

During last night's argument, while he and Dana walked along Paris-Plage, too late for the last métro, too drunk for safe conversation, he said, "I need quiet. Your life is too noisy."

Did he mean that? Where did that come from? Had four days with Chantal—long, leisurely days of conversation—led to this clamoring in his mind?

In the middle of sloppy, drunken, angry sex, the kind of sex he and Dana never had, the kind that left them raw and panting, Dana had asked, "Are you leaving me?"

"No," he assured her. "No. I love you. I'll always love you."

And now this: Chantal standing in front of him at the entrance of the métro station, her hair slipping out of its barrette so that wavy tendrils trace the lines of her long neck. Her sideways glance at him, as if to say, *I know you now. I know something's up.* Her smell. He fell asleep last night imagining the smell of jasmine and green tea, some heady mix that he yearns for as he leans toward Chantal now, kissing her on both cheeks, no handshake today. It's their last day together. In Paris.

Maybe it's Paris that has me acting like a fool, Jeremy thinks. He looks around him and again, in an instant, he has that uncanny feeling that he's seeing everything for the first time. It's the surprise of it all, the non–Los Angeles of it, the new light, the old buildings, the discovery of learning a city by walking its streets.

Immediately he's hounded by guilt, as if Dana can hear his thoughts. No, his life with her is certainly not bland. It's not her. It's Los Angeles. It's Hollywood. He'd feel this way if he were suddenly transported to the Teton mountains.

But Chantal would not be standing in front of him in the Teton mountains.

"Our last day," Chantal says in French. "Are you ready?"

There are so many things he can say. No, I am not ready for my French lessons to end. Yes, I am ready for you. No, I am not ready for my life to change. Yes, I am ready for you. No, I am not ready for Lindy, my stepdaughter, who showed up unexpectedly at the apartment last night with a newly shaved head. I am not ready for another night with the insufferable film crew.

"*Oui,*" he says. "*Je suis prêt.*"

The French tutor smiles her beguiling smile, and Jeremy relaxes for the first time this morning.

They are standing outside the métro in the Fifth Arrondissement. Each morning they meet at a different métro station. Chantal and Jeremy stroll the streets of Paris while they speak French. Jeremy likes this system and wonders if Chantal always does this with her students or if she invented this program when she first met Jeremy, four days ago, and saw that he was more comfortable while in motion. If only I could have learned while on the move when I was a kid, he thinks. I might have liked a walking school.

He doesn't doubt that Chantal would be capable of knowing this about him in a few short hours. In these four days, she has found out that he likes to talk about architecture, about wood, about politics and literature. And so she has steered their conversations as well as their meanderings around Paris, suiting his needs without ever seeming to ask him what he would like to do.

Yesterday's brilliant summer sky is gone and clouds have moved in. Chantal carries an umbrella. The air is thick with humidity and rich odors.

"We will start at the market," Chantal says in French. "I will introduce you to the language of food."

Jeremy had not told Chantal that he loves to cook. He smiles at her and nods, pleased to be at her side.

"I bought my husband a beautiful French girl for our anniversary," Dana told their dinner companions last night.

"Not exactly," Jeremy added.

"I wanted him to come with me on this shoot," Dana explained, leaning conspiratorially toward the men and women at the table, her voice lowered as if sharing a secret. But they were the last patrons at the restaurant. Dana hadn't finished filming until after ten o'clock. They began their dinner at 10:30 or so, and it was now almost one in the morning. The waiters lingered at the doorway to the kitchen, anxious to leave. "It's our tenth anniversary—I wasn't going to spend it alone in Paris."

Dana is never alone. She has fellow actors and directors and agents and fans, so many fans that she is even recognized in this foreign city.

"I just finished a restoration project in Santa Barbara," Jeremy said. "I was happy to come along."

He cursed himself for feeling the need to remind their dinner companions that he too works, that he does have a life—and an artistic one at that. He doesn't just follow Dana around from one movie location to the next. But they paid no attention to him. They waited to hear about the beautiful French girl. Jeremy wished he were back at the hotel with Dana, in bed, alone at last.

"But what could he do all day in Paris while I'm filming?" Dana said to the group. "Well, Pascale gave me the name of a language school and I set him up with a full week of private tutoring. While I'm working he's learning the language of love with someone named Chantal."

She spread the name open like it too was a gift: "Chant-a-a-al."

"Not quite," Jeremy said. He's accustomed to his wife's stories, the way they grow. By tomorrow night Chantal might be the most beautiful woman in all of France. "We haven't yet discussed love," he explained.

Everyone was charmed.

"Thank God I trust you the way I do," Dana added.

"My stepdaughter would like to meet us for coffee," Jeremy tells
Chantal, in French, as they walk toward the steep hill of rue
Mouffetard. Jeremy can see the long line of food stalls ahead; he
can hear a man calling out, *"Cerises! Melons!"* Jeremy can understand Chantal's French with surprising ease, but he's lost with
heavy accents or rapid-fire patter.

"How old is your stepdaughter?"

"She's twenty," Jeremy says. "She left me a note this morning. I haven't even talked to her yet. She arrived sometime in the
middle of the night. If you think it would be too difficult—"

"No, not at all," Chantal says. "I'd love to meet her."

Jeremy glances at Chantal. She is poised, elegant, a proper
young Parisian woman. Suddenly he can't imagine her next to
wild Lindy. He hears loud voices ahead and turns his attention
to the market. He's not sure he wants to enter the noise and
tumult—for the first time he considers suggesting something
other than what Chantal has planned. A quiet street, someplace
they can talk without shouting. They might talk about their lives,
something they haven't done all week. Who is this woman? He
wants to know her—where she is from, where she lives now,
what she wants in her life.

Why shouldn't they talk about matters of the heart? In
French! He has always known that his French is good, but he's
not one to take risks, to try out unsure sentences on strangers.
And he doesn't like to make a fool of himself. With Chantal his
sentences seem to come out fully formed, as if he has been wait-

ing for twenty-five years, since his college French classes, to speak with this woman.

And of course, whenever they come to Paris, it's Dana who speaks. She had spent a year at the Sorbonne and fell in love with an Algerian man who returned with her to UCLA, living in her dorm room until her parents found out and disposed of him. Dana even *looks* French, or maybe it's the short skirts and black tights she always wears. She urges Jeremy to speak in French when they shop or dine, but he finds that it takes too long to find the right words. Eventually she jumps in and helps him out.

"Will you buy me a pastry, *monsieur*?" Chantal asks, and that's the first stall they come to, a baker's table, with pastries laid out in delectable rows—croissants, brioches, *pains aux amandes, pains au chocolat, éclairs, palmiers.*

"What would you like?" he asks, turning to Chantal. It feels surprisingly intimate, this simple act.

She looks for a moment and then points.

"Deux palmiers, s'il vous plaît," he says to the baker. There is no hesitation in his voice—he doesn't sound like the tourist who's unsure if he's said it right. Usually when he speaks French, his voice is too soft and he is asked to repeat himself. Simple, he thinks. It's just a question of confidence.

The baker is a man his own age, too slim to be very interested in his own creations. He eyes Chantal and then smiles at Jeremy. Jeremy needs no translation here.

He pays for the pastries and turns to Chantal.

She looks away. Did she see the other man's appreciative glance? She is suddenly shy with Jeremy.

"Tell me about the food," Jeremy says, pointing up the street at the stalls lining the narrow road. "We'll talk about my stepdaughter later."

He feels oddly unfaithful talking about Lindy. She belongs to his life with Dana. And she's complicated. She dropped out of school, stopped talking to her mother, and pulled Jeremy into her secrets. The fact that she appeared some time in the middle of the night, unannounced, and newly bald, has him worried. He has no idea what to expect from her. Easier to talk about eggplants and olallieberries.

Jeremy hears music and looks past the baker's table. How could he have missed the sounds of the accordions? Again he hears the shouts of vendors hawking their fruits and vegetables, and in the mix, the sweet voice of someone singing. There's too much to hear, too much to see. He focuses his eyes on a small circle of people gathered in a tiny square at the foot of rue Mouffetard. Three men play accordions, a woman stands with a microphone and sings, and in the middle of the circle a couple dances.

"Let's go watch," Jeremy says, and he leads Chantal through the market crowd to the performers. He glances at Chantal while they wrangle for space at the edge of the circle; her eyes are wide, a smile spreads across her face. He feels as if he's created this Édith Piaf world.

The dancing couple is elderly—early seventies, he'd guess. And yet they move nimbly, gracefully, keeping perfect time with the music. They're both tall and slim and look as if they've spent a lifetime in each other's arms, spinning, bending, pulling out and back again. The woman is dressed in a fifties-style dress, with a full skirt that billows while she twirls. She wears shoes with straps that lace around her ankles. The man wears all white— a white cap, white shirt, white slacks, white shoes. He's dapper and delicate.

A woman walks the perimeter of the circle, handing out

sheets of paper. Jeremy takes one: it's a song sheet. Already, he hears voices joining in song.

"Do they do this every day?" he asks Chantal.

"I've never seen it," she says. "It's beautiful."

Another couple steps out to dance. They're younger, less talented, but thoroughly pleased with themselves. And a woman with an enormous floppy hat joins the circle to dance on her own, her arms gracefully floating in the air around her, perhaps circling an imaginary partner.

"Would you like to dance?" Jeremy asks Chantal.

"I'm a terrible dancer," she says.

"That's impossible."

He takes her hand and steps into the circle. He places his hand on the narrow curve of her waist and feels her fingers lightly land on his shoulder. He lifts his other hand, and she curls her fingers around his. She looks up at him with a nervous smile.

He begins to move her around the small space, listening to the sound of the accordions, testing her response to his gentle pressure on her back. She looks worried, unsure, and glances down at her feet.

"Look at *me*," he says. He knows how to dance—not skillfully, like the man in white. But he knows how to hear the music and move in its rhythm. This is what he does best: not talking, not storytelling or confessions or late-night arguments. He knows how bodies talk to each other.

He sees Chantal's worried frown disappear—he lets her spin and sees a smile stretch across her face.

He imagines her in bed and pulls her closer. The music stops. She steps away.

"*Merci*," she says, but she doesn't look at him.

She steps off the makeshift dance floor and into the crowd of spectators.

He waits a moment before following her. It would be so easy, he thinks, to take her hand and pull her back. *One more dance. Give yourself up to the music. Give yourself up to me.*

But he thinks of Dana, of her body under his in bed, of the hunger in her eyes. He feels something stir inside him—desire, need, frustration—whatever it is, he's in love with his wife. He's just spending the day with a French tutor. *Get back to the lesson,* he tells himself.

He follows Chantal and they wind their way through the crowd. A new song has begun, something about *le petit vin blanc.* New dancers take the stage. But Chantal's on the move and soon they're back on rue Mouffetard, and the noise of the marketplace drowns out the accordions.

They walk along the row of stalls that line both sides of the narrow street, most covered with colorful awnings, the tables piled high with fresh vegetables, lush fruit, bowls of olives, a profusion of flowers. Chantal discusses the cuts of meat, the varieties of fish, the classifications of cheese. Jeremy asks good questions—he wants to understand why the quality of the cheese is so superior in France, why there are vegetables and fruits he has never seen before, and what does one do with ramp leaves?

Chantal unbuttons her cardigan sweater—the market is crowded and hot. People bump into them and push them against each other. She is wearing a pale pink blouse. Jeremy realizes that she has never worn any color before. All of her clothing seems to come in shades of gray and black.

She looks at him; his eyes are on her neck. He looks away quickly.

"Tell me about olive oil," he says. In front of them are a dozen bottles of olive oil, and a beefy man urges them to taste one. Jeremy dips a wedge of bread into a small bowl of oil. When he tastes the oil on his tongue he realizes that it is the first thing he has eaten today and he is suddenly ravenous. He tastes all of the different selections of oil, dunking slices of baguette into each bowl, and Chantal laughs at his eager appetite. He then buys two bottles of the best oil, one for Chantal and one that he will take home with him. The taste will always remind him of this odd breakfast with Chantal.

By the time they leave the market, they are both carrying plastic bags on their arms, as if they had set out on a shopping spree rather than a French lesson. Chantal tucks a baguette into her tote bag. They have not spoken about lunch, but Jeremy imagines a *pique-nique* in one of the hidden parks they have passed on their many walks.

They turn down a side street—a kind of medieval pedestrian alley—and in an instant the noise of the market dissipates. They are quiet for a moment and then Chantal tells him that they will walk to the Jardin des Plantes, where there is a museum of natural history. She thinks he will find it interesting.

"Yes, I'm sure I will," he says, pleased with the idea.

On their second day together they walked through a neighborhood filled with antiques stores so that Chantal could teach him the language of furniture and jewelry and art. When she saw that he paid close attention to the kinds of wood in the best of the period furniture, she arranged for the two of them to speak with a man who restores antiques. They stood in the charming clutter of the old man's atelier, with the man's low, steady voice in his ear and the odors of the wood and solvents and Chantal's fragrant perfume in his nose. The late-afternoon light filtered through the small, high windows of the shop, and Jeremy thought: I'm happy here. This is where I belong.

What a strange thought for him to have. He has never wanted to live abroad.

He has lived in California all his life and only began to travel when he met Dana eleven years ago. He's a homebody; he wants his dog and his house projects and his books and his chair by the fire. He and Dana live in Santa Monica Canyon, and he only joins her for Hollywood events when she insists, which luckily she rarely does. He owns a couple of suits but lives in his work clothes. When he spends days on a project out of the house—restoring something that can't be transported to his shop—he feels unsettled, as if he has stepped out of his skin. He can't wait to get home in the evenings. So why should he now feel like he belongs in a foreign city?

He thinks about what has happened in this week that he's spent with Chantal. He has looked at Paris with new eyes. It's not only his view of his surroundings that has grown sharper, more vivid. He feels different in his own skin. He's someone else when he speaks French—someone more intriguing, more mysterious. It's invigorating, as if he is capable of anything in this new place.

He could take a woman's hand and lead her onto the dance floor.

"While we walk to the museum," Chantal says, "tell me about your stepdaughter."

Jeremy wishes for a moment that they could walk in silence. But that's absurd—this is a French lesson, after all.

He likes having Chantal next to him, her tall, slim body such a surprise to him after years of walking with Dana, who is petite and compact, a kind of miniature woman who seems to be in motion even when she is standing still. He shouldn't compare his wife with his French tutor—it's not as if he's dating this young woman—but he's become unaccustomed to the attentions of a woman. She's paid, he reminds himself. His wife is paying her to be with him. The thought turns his mood sour in a quick second.

"Lindy is my wife's daughter," Jeremy says. "I came into her life when she was nine."

"And you are close," Chantal says. "I can see something in your face when you speak of her."

"I love her," he says, simply. It is true. He had not wanted children, and when Dana told him she had a child he had briefly considered ending the relationship. He was thirty-five when they met and every woman he dated wanted to have a baby—immediately—regardless of love or compatibility. Dana told him that she didn't want another child, but that she hoped he would want this ready-made family. Lindy was a child-sized version of her mother, the same kind of radiance, the same kind of charm. He was doubly smitten.

And over the years he learned to be a father to the girl. Her own father was a portfolio manager, specializing in international real estate—he was always in Singapore, Tokyo, Sydney. Lindy had a room full of souvenirs but no picture of her father on her bureau. Instead she framed one photo of the three of them taken in Costa Rica four or five years ago. They are rafting the wild Pacuare River, bundled in orange life vests, the thick green jungle surrounding them. Dana is in the front of the raft, her eyes open wide with astonishment that some drop in the river is about to claim them, and behind her, sixteen-year-old Lindy leans into Jeremy, both of them smiling with pure delight.

Jeremy tells Chantal about Lindy's recent rebellion—when

she dropped out of college she disappeared for a while, sending her mother into a fury. Jeremy received an email from Lindy saying "I'm safe. I need to do this. Tell Mom not to get too wigged out. I love you." Jeremy can't translate "wigged out," so he says the words in English and Chantal seems to understand. Funny. He doesn't even know if his tutor speaks English.

"I think she needs to find her own path," Jeremy says. "Her mother is very successful. I think that makes it hard for her to know how to define herself."

"Does she want to be an actress too?" Chantal asks.

"Yes," Jeremy says. "I can't tell her not to try."

"Is she talented?"

Jeremy nods. For a moment he thinks ahead of himself, in a rush of translated words that bump into one another. "I don't know the word in French. She has talent but she doesn't have the aggression—no, the *spirit*—I can't explain it." Aggression, he thinks. What an ugly word for what drives his wife. *Drive*, that's it. But he's too bewildered to try to explain himself.

"She's only twenty," Chantal says. "Most of us do not have direction at that age."

"How old are you?" Jeremy asks. The minute he says it, he wants to take it back. It sounds like they're on some kind of date.

"Twenty-eight," Chantal says, unruffled. "And still searching for my own direction."

"I always knew what I wanted," Jeremy tells her. "I wanted to work with wood even as a child. I had a first job out of college with a contractor. But I didn't want to build new things. I learned that very quickly. I'm drawn to old things, broken things. I take great pleasure in bringing them back to their original beauty."

Chantal smiles at him. "I am not surprised," she says.

"And you?" Jeremy asks. "What are you drawn to?"

Chantal doesn't answer for a moment. Finally, she shrugs. "Language. Words. No, not teaching. Perhaps one day I'll write something."

"Poetry?"

She shakes her head. "I tell stories to my nephew when I visit him. About a dog who speaks many languages. It's not very poetic. But it's a good story."

"Children's books."

Chantal shrugs. "I'm just dreaming."

"You should. We all need to have our dreams."

"For now, I pay the bills."

Jeremy winces. He's paying her bills. A rude reminder that this is not a date. Is he so out of practice that he can no longer tell when a woman might be interested in him? Before he met Dana he knew that he could win a woman if he wanted to—he simply paid attention. And he was good-looking. Now, ten years later, he assumes he is still good-looking, even if his hair is peppered with gray and his body is thicker. Women still glance in his direction, and sometimes try to charm him. He has never responded to any of those flirtations—he has fallen into a life he never expected, with a woman and child he loves.

Nothing has changed, he tells himself. It's the week in Paris that has so disoriented him. It's the fight with Dana last night— a rare fight—that has him on edge.

They had walked through Paris at two in the morning, passing up the offer of a ride from Pascale, the director. "We'll walk," Dana shouted to her crowd of admirers from across the street. "I want to be alone with my handsome man. Now all of you go away!"

After a block or two, she took Jeremy's arm and leaned into him.

"This is what I want," she said. "You."

"Then why do you fill our lives with everyone else?" he asked.

"That's work, my love. You know that." Her voice was sleepy and drunk; she pressed herself against him.

"I shouldn't come on these film shoots," Jeremy said. "I feel like I lose you every time."

"You've never said that before."

"We want such different things."

"No, we don't. We both want this."

She was right. He knew that whenever they were alone together, whenever their bodies found each other in bed, whenever they sat across from each other at the small table in their garden in the canyon and shared a bottle of wine. But at the restaurant earlier that evening, Jeremy had felt as if he'd married a movie star. He wanted Dana, not the star attraction.

"I have a blister on my heel," Dana said, reaching down and rubbing her ankle. "I can't walk in these damn things."

"Let's find a cab."

"No, let's walk. I drank too much. We can walk along the quai. Paris-Plage is set up for the summer. We'll walk on the boardwalk. We'll build a sand castle. We'll pretend we're at the beach."

"It's a long walk. You'll kill your feet."

"I don't care. Tomorrow I'll have a hangover and broken feet. Tonight I'll have my head on your shoulder."

Jeremy wrapped his arm around her.

"Don't get tired of me," she said quietly.

"I'm tired of the noise," he said.

"What noise?" She stopped and pulled away from him. Her face hardened and she pulled off her shoe, hopped on one foot, bending the back of the shoe.

"You'll ruin the shoe."

"What noise? What are you talking about?"

"I need quiet. Your life is too noisy."

She threw the shoe at him. He wanted to laugh—she looked small and furious—and he caught the shoe as if catching a grenade. He tossed it back at her.

"This happens a few times a year," she said, her voice too loud in the dark street. A window slammed shut in the apartment beside them. "I shoot a film, get crazy busy, and then I come home and it's all over and we have our life together. This isn't my life. It's my job. You're my life, goddamn it! What are you talking about?"

He stared at her, amazed. He imagined her onscreen, those big emotions, those wild eyes, the husky voice. "You don't have to scream," he said softly.

"Yes, I do!" she shouted. She stuffed her foot back in the shoe and stormed off. He followed her.

Even off the screen, he was married to drama, he thought. He felt weary and angry with himself for starting something out of nothing. He imagined Chantal, somewhere in Paris, reading a book by the window, hearing the angry shouts of a married couple on the street below. She would quietly close the window.

"There it is," Chantal says, pointing to the museum up ahead.

"*Bon*," Jeremy says, and they cross the street to the Muséum national d'histoire Naturelle. It's a renovated old building, par-

tially covered with a bold blue banner announcing all the exhibition halls in the Jardin des Plantes. Apparently, they're headed
to the Grande Galerie de l'évolution. Beyond the museum Jeremy sees long stretches of green lawn and well-tended gardens.

Inside, a double line of schoolchildren wait to get in. The
teachers stand at the ticket booth, arguing with the agent, while
the children stand obediently, shuffling their feet, talking quietly
to one another.

"American children would be running all over the place,"
Jeremy says. "This is amazing. The teachers don't even have to
scold them."

"Oh, we follow so many rules," Chantal says, "until we have
had our fill. By the time we reach twenty we rebel like wild
horses on short leads."

"And you? Did you rebel?"

"No," Chantal says. "Not yet."

They both smile, and when she turns around quickly the
baguette in her bag smacks Jeremy on his head. The kids burst
out laughing and Chantal looks back at Jeremy, her face a sudden pink.

"I'm so sorry."

"I'll survive," Jeremy says. "If I have a black eye tomorrow
I'll have to invent a much better story."

"Tell your wife I punched you," Chantal says.

"Did I give you good reason?"

"Oh, yes," she says.

And then she hurries off to buy tickets. The schoolchildren
have filed into the museum ahead of them and she is next in
line.

Jeremy glances at his watch. Ten forty-five. They will have

only forty-five minutes before they meet Lindy at the café. He calls Lindy on his cell phone. She doesn't answer, but he's connected to her voice mail.

"*Bonjour, chérie,*" he says happily. She'll be impressed. Like her mother, she speaks French with ease. Good private-school training, a summer program in Aix-en-Provence during high school. Jeremy continues with his message in French. "Meet us at the mosque. It's across from the entrance to the Jardin des Plantes in the Fifth. You can't miss it." He had noticed it on his walk here with Chantal. "There's a tearoom inside. I can't wait to see you, sweetheart. I peeked in this morning while you were sleeping. I—" He can't think of how to refer to the bald head. Her new haircut? Her latest rebellion? He coughs and then hangs up as if their connection was lost.

He didn't mention the shaved scalp to Dana. She'll be furious.

"*On y va,*" Chantal says. She takes his arm, something she has never done before, and leads him into the grand entrance of the museum.

The minute they step through the door, Jeremy takes a deep breath. It's a spectacular space, vast and open, dark yet eerily beckoning. On the ground floor of the central exhibition space he sees the march of animals, life-size, regal and elegant—elephants, giraffes, zebras. He's awed by their size, their numbers, their beauty. He and Chantal move forward and look up. The four-story space is open in the middle as if the animals need room to breathe.

Jeremy is distracted by the light touch of Chantal's hand on his forearm. It's as if all his energy and attention has rushed, like blood, to this one part of his anatomy. His skin feels warm, and he imagines her hand making an impression on his skin, as if he

were made of clay. She is saying something and he hasn't been
listening.

"I'm sorry," he says. "What did you say?"

She looks at him, surprised. Of course, he always pays such
close attention.

"There was a word I didn't understand," he says, finding a
feeble excuse. "And so I got lost."

"I will find you," Chantal says, smiling. "Perhaps you were
lost with the penguins?"

He looks to the right—there's a display of penguins staring
at him.

Her hand leaves his arm and she steps toward the magnifi-
cent march of the animals. She gestures toward them and names
them all, slowly, as if Jeremy is not only lost but a little slow.

He laughs. "I feel like I belong with the schoolchildren."

"You are not well enough behaved," Chantal says.

"That's not about to change now," he tells her.

But that's not true. Jeremy has not behaved badly in years.
He has been a perfect partner to Dana since he met her. That
first time—a chance meeting—changed him; he knew that by
the end of the day, when he told her: "Come home with me."

He had been working on a house in Bel Air, restoring a library that had been built in 1901 and neglected for more than a
century. The owner of the house had warned him: A film crew
was shooting a scene in the house, but the library was off-limits
to them. No one told Dana that, and she had wandered in while
the director was working on a scene that didn't include her.

She had walked around the library quietly, and finally stood
beside Jeremy's ladder, watching him. He was fitting a delicately
carved cornice onto the built-in breakfront bookcase. He had
replicated the piece from old photos. It had taken weeks to

shape, carve, and finish the intricate pierced form from a piece of mahogany.

He glanced at her, nodded, and returned his attention to his work.

"That's very beautiful," she said finally. "Do you live here?"

"No," he said. "An actor lives here. Someone with enough money and enough good taste to save this place instead of tearing it down."

"You don't know who the actor is?"

"I don't know much about that world," Jeremy told her.

He noticed how her smile grew.

"I'm Dana Hurley," she said.

"Jeremy Diamond," he said, stepping down from the ladder.

"Would you like a glass of champagne?" she asked. "I can get it for you. Or something to eat?"

"You're on the film crew?" he asked.

"I'm an actress," she said.

"Somehow I bet I'm the only man in America who hasn't heard of you," he said.

"Can I hide here with you?" she asked, still smiling.

"Yes," he said.

He set his chisel and wooden mallet aside and wiped his hands. They sat in the two club chairs by the bay windows and talked for a long time.

"This could be our house," Dana said at one point.

"I would build us a much nicer house," Jeremy told her.

He discovered in the first weeks after meeting her that he was more than ready to give up short-term relationships and one-night stands. Dana offered so much more than all of those many women he used to date. And then there was something new: real love, responsibility, taking care of someone. Fatherhood—that,

too, changed him and made him want nothing else than what
he had.

"What are those?" Jeremy asks Chantal, interrupting his own
thoughts. He'll be the good student again, pointing at some
ratty thing nipping at the heels of a graceful deer.

Chantal offers vocabulary words that he'll never use. He
thinks of his dog at home, a pet sitter taking care of her and
promising long walks in the hills. He needs a long walk in the
hills. He's been city-bound too long. These animals remind him
that he needs air, space, motion. Everything about this beautiful
museum is wrong. The animals are trapped inside.

"Let's move outside," Chantal says.

Jeremy glances at her. Does she read him so easily?

"The grounds are beautiful," she says, as if he needs further
urging.

She's right, and Jeremy breathes more easily. Once they're
through the front door, the Jardin des Plantes spreads out before
them. They walk through gardens that represent different ecosys-
tems while Chantal offers the French names for different flowers, trees, wild ferns. On a central path in the large park, the
children follow their teachers in two straight lines, like Noah's
animals. The air is thick with woodsy smells, and Jeremy remembers the evening after the rafting trip in Costa Rica. They
had camped in the jungle along the side of the river, and the
river guides had cooked fish wrapped in banana leaves on an
open campfire. Lindy told Jeremy that she had a crush on their
river guide, a wiry, dark-skinned young man who had taught
them to spin the boat in the rapids. "Don't tell Mom I like him,"
she had said. "I won't," he told her. It was the first time she had
offered a secret. He held it close to him, an extraordinary gift.

"I want to live in the country one day," Chantal says.

Jeremy is surprised. She has told him so little about her life.

"Why not move?" he asks.

"My boyfriend loves Paris," she says. "Though he told me this morning he's thinking of moving to London."

"And you?" He tries to ignore the twinge of jealousy. Of course she has a boyfriend. And what does it matter?

"I spend a lot of time in this garden. This is my favorite spot in the city."

Jeremy looks around with different eyes. He wants to know why she loves this particular garden and yet he won't ask. He thinks he might come to know Chantal if he knows this garden.

"Will you move to London with this boyfriend?" Jeremy asks.

"I saw him kissing another woman this morning," Chantal says. "Maybe I deserve a better boyfriend."

The sky darkens and then flashes white. A growl of thunder follows immediately.

"Let's go inside," Chantal says.

"No. We'll duck under the trees," Jeremy tells her. "Let's watch the storm."

She looks at him, surprised, and then her face lights up. They can hear the high-pitched shrieks of the children, who dash back into the closest exhibition hall as the skies open.

Jeremy wraps his hand around Chantal's upper arm and leads her deeper into the woods. They step over a low fence—a sign reads INTERDIT!—and under the wide canopy of trees. The rain hits the back of Jeremy's neck in sharp little stabs. And then they're protected, the thick shelf of leaves and branches above them sheltering them from the downpour that surrounds them.

It is wild. The sky is almost as black as if day had changed to night. Peals of thunder roll across the sky, bumping into one another without a break. And the rain! It comes down in solid sheets, loud, crashing on the paths, the lawn, the tree canopy above them.

Chantal presses against Jeremy's side as if frightened. But he sees her face—she is thrilled by the storm. He smiles to himself, glad that they didn't run for cover.

And finally there are no words—even the jumble of French and English in Jeremy's mind slows and quiets. There is only this: the lashing of wind at the trees, the pounding of the rain on the earth, the clamor of the sky.

Jeremy can smell Chantal's shampoo—something like tangerines. He breathes her in.

He made love with Dana last night when they returned from their street fight sometime after three in the morning, having walked all the way from the Marais to their hotel near Saint-Sulpice church. She had turned to him as soon as they climbed into bed.

"I need you," she whispered, and he glared at her. Did she need sex or him? He pushed her back on the bed and, pinning her shoulders down, climbed on top of her.

"What do you need? Say it," he said.

"You."

"Sex," he said.

"You."

"You don't need me," he said. He leaned close to her and she reached up for his mouth—their kiss was full of hunger and rage. They tore at each other, tangling themselves in the sheets, and at one point Jeremy felt Dana's mouth on his neck, her teeth sharp. They turned each other over and pushed each other back, each fighting to overpower the other. They had never done this, never been rough or scrappy in bed. Their lovemaking was always tender, intimate; their eyes always locked on each other. This time, they barely looked at each other.

When Jeremy came, his orgasm seemed to go on for a long time. And then Dana didn't wait for him to pleasure her—she took his hand and pressed it between her legs. She held it there and moved against him, her body scrambling for release. When she found it she called out his name.

"Are you all right?" he asked her, when they slid into their sleeping positions, his body curled against her back, his arm wrapped around her and curled between her breasts.

"I need to come home to you," she said softly.

The storm stops as suddenly as it began. Chantal moves away from Jeremy's side. It makes him catch his breath, as if he might stumble without the weight of her against him.

"*Merci,*" she says simply.

"*Avec plaisir,*" he tells her, smiling.

"*Regarde,*" she says, pointing out toward the expanse of gardens. New light spreads across the lush greenery, bouncing off drops of rain as if electric. Everything looks newly sprouted, astonishingly different. It's as if he hadn't even seen the garden before.

She does not name what they are looking at.

They step carefully through the wet grass and over the small fence and back onto the path. Chantal lifts her closed umbrella and laughs. "What a silly thing it is."

"I hate to leave," Jeremy says with real regret, "but we need to meet my daughter."

"Of course," Chantal says.

"I asked Lindy to meet us across the street at the mosque." He pauses, searching her face. "If that's okay with you."

"That's a very good plan," she says. "I would have suggested it myself."

Jeremy feels a swelling of pride, as if he has written an A paper. *A schoolboy's crush,* he thinks. *What a fool.*

And yet there is some comfort in naming these odd sensations swirling through him today. As if now he can put it in its place. It is translatable, after all.

He wonders suddenly: Did Lindy sleep with the river guide that night? The next day, at the airport in San José, she had sobbed before they boarded the plane, and she wouldn't talk to her mother. When Dana went to the bathroom, Lindy whispered to Jeremy, "I want to stay with Paco. I can't leave him." Jeremy kissed the top of her head. "Is this love?" he asked, smiling. "Of course it's love!" she shouted, and stormed off.

Why does naming a thing give it so much power? Jeremy wonders.

Chantal glances at her watch. "It is almost eleven-thirty. I am the only person in Paris who is always on time. Let's not ruin my good record."

That, too, pleases Jeremy. Of course, Dana is always late—the meeting ran over, the photographer didn't show up, the director demanded twenty takes of the same damn scene. He brings a book with him whenever he sets out to meet her. And he expects to wait. When she finally arrives, he usually forgets any annoyance as soon as she begins to tell him about her day. Her days are filled with stories. He works quietly with his wood and his tools and his silence. At the end of his day, it's as if Dana opens the window and lets the world in.

They walk quickly through the gardens. Jeremy feels breathless, as if the storm might reappear at any moment. But no, the sky is light, the clouds gone. Chantal has shifted the bags on her shoulders and now, instead of feeling her body brush against his, it is only her tote bag that bumps his hip as they hurry along.

"Jeremy!" Lindy shouts when they reach the gates of the Jardin des Plantes. She dashes across the street and throws herself in his arms before he even gets a good look at the girl. She squeezes tight and he finds himself laughing. His child. There is no question she is his, even though she has only spent half her life with him. She has chosen him, which is even better than what most dads get.

"You're beautiful," he says when words come. He holds her out in front of him. It is still true: the shockingly bald head makes her green eyes even more luminous. Her smile is radiant.

"*En français!*" she scolds. And then she turns to Chantal and offers her hand. "*Je m'appelle Lindy.*"

"Chantal. *Enchantée.*"

"Does he really speak French?" she asks conspiratorially, in French, as if Jeremy is not there.

"Very well," Chantal says. "As do you."

"*Bof.* I've forgotten my French. I need practice—I need a French boyfriend. That would help."

"You can have mine," Chantal says.

Jeremy looks at her—she is smiling effortlessly. Jeremy feels as if he's lost control of this conversation. He doesn't speak girl talk in any language.

"Shall we find the tearoom?" he asks in French.

"Oh, you sound different in French!" Lindy exclaims.

"How so?" he asks.

"I don't know. You're so—sexy."

"Apparently I'm not sexy in English," Jeremy explains to Chantal.

"No, not that," Lindy says. "You're like someone I don't know. You could be anyone."

"Not your stepfather."

"My stepfather wouldn't be out on the town with a beautiful young Frenchwoman."

Chantal looks away quickly.

"Lindy," Jeremy says, then stops. The girl's smile looks devious. But Lindy is never devious. She is so truly an unaffected girl, even with all the flash and glamour of her mother's life thrust upon her. She is always unfailingly honest.

"This is a French lesson," he explains, his voice low and serious.

"Well, of course it is," Lindy says.

They cross the street and enter the mosque. It's a Moorish building with an impressive minaret, all white on the outside, coolly inviting. They pass through the outside café and enter the inner courtyard. It's beautifully tiled, with tables set around fig trees and fountains. Arabic music plays in the background; Jeremy can smell incense. He feels transported to Morocco and remembers a trip with Dana to shoot a movie in Marrakesh. One evening they walked through the medina, and even though Dana wore jeans and a tunic, every man turned his head to watch her pass. Jeremy never relaxed his guard, watching and waiting for trouble while Dana shopped for trinkets, oblivious to the stir of male attention around her. By the end of the evening he was exhausted but oddly pleased. It was his job; she needed him there.

"Une table pour trois, monsieur?" the waiter asks. Jeremy looks up, surprised. The young man seems inordinately pleased with the sight of these two young women at Jeremy's side.

"Oui. S'il vous plaît."

The man ushers them to a table at the edge of the courtyard. They're next to a fountain, and suddenly the noise—of the cascade of water, the incantatory music, and, oddly, the squawk of a bird trapped inside the room—makes Jeremy feel claustrophobic. He should have chosen to sit outside.

The waiter says something in rapid-fire French and Jeremy looks at Chantal, completely lost.

"No," she tells the waiter. "We'll only be having drinks."

They settle into their chairs and tuck their bags of cheese and fruit and meat under the table. Jeremy notices that the baguette is soggy from the rain. He looks up and sees Lindy, eyes on him.

"Tell me about your adventures," he says to her.

"Well," she begins, but then the waiter is there, speaking too quickly for him to understand. Is it the Arabic accent? Too much noise? There's a pause. Chantal orders tea. He does the same. Lindy orders a *citron pressé*.

"Spain? Portugal?" he prompts when the waiter is gone.

"Tell me about your French lessons," Lindy says. "What are you learning? French conjugations? The imperfect tense?"

She's looking back and forth between Chantal and him. She's got a mischievous gleam in her eyes, as if she's taunting him.

"Lindy," he says, his voice low.

"Jeremy and I have conversations about the things we see as we walk around Paris. I teach him new vocabulary. I correct his mistakes. I encourage him to practice what he already knows."

Chantal is remarkably calm, as if she is often confronted by irrational twenty-year-old bald daughters. Jeremy begins to relax.

"What fun," Lindy says, as if it's not fun at all.

"Your mother set up these lessons for me," Jeremy explains. He doesn't mention that it's an anniversary gift.

"How gallant of her."

Gallant, Jeremy thinks. Lindy's French surprises him. She, too, sounds like someone else, someone more sophisticated. Someone with an edge.

"Tell us about your travels," Jeremy urges.

"Well, here I am," Lindy says. "All roads lead home."

"But you're not home," Jeremy says.

"I'm with you," Lindy tells him. "That's home."

He reaches out and places his hand over hers. She flinches but doesn't take her hand away. He sees her glance at Chantal and back again, quickly.

The waiter arrives and sets tea in front of them, lemonade in front of Lindy. He makes a grand gesture of pouring tea for Chantal but leaves Jeremy to serve himself.

"Did you see your mother this morning?" Jeremy asks.

Dana was still sleeping when he left for his French lesson. Her filming doesn't begin until late this afternoon—they're shooting evening scenes on the Pont des Arts. He has promised to come watch tonight, something he doesn't often do. But tomorrow is their anniversary and he needs to make up for last night's fight. Before Lindy called to say she would arrive in the middle of the night, they had thought they would take a train to Chantilly and explore the château. But now Dana wants to stay in Paris, just the three of them, roaming the city. "I haven't had a chance to walk the streets of Paris," she had said last night. "You're the one who's having all the fun."

"Mom was sleeping," Lindy says. "My mother is an actress," she tells Chantal.

"So I've heard," Chantal says.

"You've mentioned her?" Lindy asks Jeremy.

"Chantal taught me the words for director and cinematographer and film editor," Jeremy tells her. "Apparently I know more words about food than I do about film."

"Mom could teach you those words."

Jeremy looks at the teacup in front of him. He has the uneasy feeling that his French lesson has ended. He and Chantal have worked until three every day. Should he let her go early? But today is his last day with her. He wants to start over. He would tell Lindy that he can't meet her until late afternoon, that he's busy all day. But of course, he's never been too busy for his daughter.

"Alors," Lindy says. "Mom was sleeping and I didn't want to wake her. Her note said that we should meet her at the Pont des Arts at six this evening."

"We'll watch them film a couple of scenes," Jeremy says. "Should be fun." He's lying; it's never fun. It's slow and boring, and each scene is so out of context that it's hard to know what's actually going on. Lindy usually hates film shoots unless a sexy young actor is on the set. Even then, she resents that her mother is more often the object of the young man's attention than she is.

Last summer, Lindy decided she wanted to be a theater actress. It's more serious, she said. It has more substance, more weight. Jeremy worries that it's even harder to succeed in the theater. He wishes his daughter would find something less daunting, something that is not filled with rejection and criticism and ego-driven competitors pushing you aside. Lindy is not made of the same stuff as her mother, he worries.

"Will *she* come?" Lindy asks.

Jeremy looks at her, confused. She's gesturing with a nod of her head at Chantal. Will Chantal come to Dana's film shoot? Of course not.

But it's Chantal who answers. "No. I have to meet some friends when our lesson is done."

"*Quel dommage,*" Lindy says.

Jeremy wonders if something has happened to Lindy on this European trip. She has sharp edges, something he has never seen before.

The waiter appears and places a plate of little cookies in front of them. He says something to Chantal—Jeremy can't understand a word he says. Did they order cookies? Is the waiter showing off for Chantal and Lindy? Chantal thanks him. Jeremy sips his tea. He's surprised by its sweetness.

When the waiter leaves, Chantal asks Lindy where she has traveled.

"I've been in a monastery," Lindy says. "In the South of France."

Is she lying? In her emails she wrote that she had bought a Eurail pass. She and a couple of friends were traveling through Spain and Portugal. In her phone calls she talked about youth hostels and parties on the beaches and getting lost in Lisbon. When he heard lots of background noise in one phone call, she told him she was at a pizza restaurant and it was someone's birthday party. Monastery?

She won't look at him. She's telling Chantal this story. He's the stranger now, listening in.

"I dropped out of college in March. I didn't know why I was studying anymore. To learn what? Environmental science? What was I going to do with that? The literature of the sixties? Cool, but so what? I just needed to know why. I don't mean I needed to know what I was going to be when I grew up. I mean,

I needed to know why I needed to learn. To take a test? To get an A? To please Papa?"

"No," Jeremy says, interrupting her. "I never put any pressure on you—"

"Oh, it's got nothing to do with you," Lindy says, waving him off. "You're easy. You just love me no matter what."

"That's important," Chantal says. "To be loved like that."

Jeremy looks at her, and it's as if his bones settle in his body again. He needs to hear Chantal's voice, he thinks. Even Lindy's French, which is very good, makes him work too hard. He has to grapple with words, to make sure he understands what she's saying. And it's so important that he gets this, that he hears her story. For the first time, he wants to say, Let's speak in English. I don't understand. A monastery?

But he doesn't say a word. Lindy is talking again, words flying by too quickly.

"Oh, it's got nothing to do with who loves me. I have this photo of me as a child with my mother. We're sitting on a couch in our old house and she's gazing down at me with a look of pure motherly devotion. That photo? Her manager came to dinner one night and swiped the photo and cropped her face and put that adoring gaze up on the cover of some stupid magazine. Now she's smiling down on the whole damn world. I'm nowhere in the picture."

"So it does have to do with love," Chantal says.

"No. It's got to do with my disappearing act. Poof, I'm gone. I'm no one, I'm everyone. I'm in college. I'm in Spain. I'm in a monastery."

"You could have talked to me about this," Jeremy says quietly.

"I needed to stop talking. That's all I did in college. Talk, talk,

talk. There are plenty of words. You can fill hours with them. And then when you stop talking, time stops. You sit there and everything opens up and you can hear your thoughts for the first time."

They stop talking. But Jeremy's mind feels like it's closing down. He can hear nothing in his brain but a low buzzing sound, as if there's static in there, a bad connection, a radio that can't pick up a station.

"I think I understand," Chantal says softly.

Jeremy looks at her beseechingly. *Help me,* he wants to say. He wants to understand his daughter. He wants to know Chantal. But it's not a question of understanding the words. He can translate each one.

In the silence, glass shatters on the other side of the courtyard, startling him. He looks up—a teacup has slipped from the waiter's hands. For a moment, he had forgotten the rest of the world, this corner of Paris, these other patrons, the sweet mint tea on the table in front of him.

"Someone told me about this monastery outside Arles. I went with a friend, but the girl left after a week. I stayed for two months." She stops and smiles. "Maybe that's why I'm talking so much."

Jeremy puts his hand on her arm.

"I'm listening," he says.

"No one ever told me I needed to be like Mom," she says simply.

She smiles at him, the sweetest smile he has seen yet. Then she turns to Chantal.

"My mother is a force of nature," she says.

Chantal nods.

"I'm not her."

She says this to Jeremy. He nods, then leans over and kisses her cheek. She smells like someone else, a grown-up woman. Maybe it's a new French soap or a perfume that she's bought. For a moment, he yearns for a younger Lindy, one without a shaved head and a flash of anger. One without such a complicated quest. But he has grown up with her. He, too, is someone else now. Ten years ago he tumbled into love with Dana and her daughter. Five years ago he thought he had it nailed—he was their rock, the one who would hold them together. And now he's not sure of anything. Only last night he pushed his chair back from the dinner table and watched Dana tell a long story about their trip to Argentina and how they climbed to the top of a mountain in the Andes and the clouds parted and the glory of the world was revealed. Jeremy listened and thought: Have I lost myself in her?

"Your monastery sounds like a very good place," he says.

"The food sucked," Lindy says in English, sounding very much like a child again. With that, she pops a cookie into her mouth.

Chantal looks at Jeremy over the rim of her teacup. Her eyes are amused, as if she has forgiven the girl her churlishness.

He wants to ask her if she is close to her parents. Does she tell them about the secrets of her heart? Even as Lindy offers him something—a glimpse of her life for the past months—she is telling him something else. I'm not yours anymore. You don't know everything about me anymore.

"When I was twenty-one I moved to an island in the Indian Ocean," Chantal says. Her eyes move from Jeremy's to Lindy's and back again. "I wanted to be something—I don't know, something other than what I was." Jeremy notices that it is the first time Chantal can't find the word she wants. "You know what I discovered living in my hippie beach commune without running water and electricity? That I am a Parisian."

Jeremy tries to imagine Chantal, with her prim cardigan sweater, her neatly wrapped umbrella, her tiny pearl earrings, this lovely composed woman—living in a tent on the beach? He smiles at the thought.

"You're laughing at me," Chantal says.

"No, not at all. Did you come home right away?"

"Not right away," Chantal explains. "But sometimes we have to run away from ourselves in order to find ourselves."

A few days ago, Chantal and Jeremy had walked through the Parc Monceau during their French lesson. A woman and a man had stood near the crepe stand, arguing loudly. *"Je suis Américaine!"* the woman yelled. *"Je suis Américaine!"* Jeremy had told Dana the story later. "What happens to your identity when you take it away from everything familiar?" he had asked. "You know yourself better," she replied assuredly.

Not me, Jeremy had thought. I know who I am when I am home in my shop. When I'm in bed with my wife. When I'm preparing dinner in my kitchen.

Already, in a few days in Paris, with a strange woman at his side, Jeremy feels like he is unmoored.

"Will you go back to the monastery?" Jeremy asks Lindy. He is a little frightened of the answer.

"No," she says lightly. "I need sex."

"Spare me," Jeremy says, in English, and both women laugh.

Lindy leans toward Chantal and says something to her under her breath. More laughter. Jeremy feels his hangover for the first time. How many bottles of wine did they all drink at dinner last night? He needs food, he needs sleep, he needs to think about something other than his daughter needing sex. He thinks that she slept with her high school boyfriend, though that relationship only lasted a month or so. Dana speculated that they were "fuck buddies" after that, a horrible thought in Jeremy's mind. Unlike most men he knows, Jeremy has always wanted love with his sex. When he knows someone in bed, he wants to know her out of bed. And when he loves her in bed, well, the rest should follow.

And here is his daughter—at twenty, beautiful and lost—looking for sex. Jeremy knows that men prey on this kind of girl and it terrifies him.

"I'm going to meet some friends," Lindy says, "at the Champ de Mars. They're having a picnic."

Jeremy remembers his imagined picnic with Chantal. Now his feet press up against the wedges of cheese, tomatoes, olives. What happens next? he wonders. When Lindy leaves?

She stands up, leans over and pecks Jeremy on both cheeks. "*À bientôt,*" she says. And then she says something in French that Jeremy doesn't understand. But Chantal smiles and shakes her head.

Lindy dashes off. Did she say something rude? Should he even ask for a translation?

"She is a beautiful girl," Chantal says.

"Thank you," Jeremy says foolishly. For of course he has nothing to do with her beauty. "I'm sorry if—"

"No, it was fine," Chantal says.

He doesn't even know what he was going to apologize for, and now it has passed. Lindy is gone. The teacups are empty. The girls have eaten their cookies. Even, somehow, the bill is paid.

"*On y va,*" Chantal says. And they are walking again.

...

Chantal has led them down to the Seine and while they stroll through the Musée de la Sculpture en Plein Air, a garden with modern sculptures dotting the landscape, they don't talk about art but about love.

"Earlier this morning I was thinking about Lindy's first love," Jeremy says. "A river guide in Costa Rica."

"How romantic," Chantal tells him.

"Oh, it turned from romance to heartbreak in a day," he explains. His mind jumps to sex with Dana last night. Pain, love, lust—sometimes it's a package deal.

"So tell me," Chantal says, "about your first love."

"My first love?"

"Please. I'd like to hear the story."

And so he tells her, in easy French, since all the words slip off his tongue—yes, it's the language of romance—while they linger by the river. A photographer is taking pictures of an Asian couple in their wedding clothes. A little girl in a pink dress with a bouquet of flowers hides behind the bride. It's a charming scene, with the stone walkway, the languid river, Notre Dame looming beyond them on the Île de la Cité. The air is thick with humidity and time seems to have slowed down.

"I met a girl at summer camp. I was thirteen. She was sixteen and much, much taller than I, with hair that fell to her waist. She wore it in one long braid that lay on her back like a thick rope. She was a swimmer and I would watch her race across our New Hampshire lake, and I thought she was the most beautiful girl in the world."

"Was it love? Or—" Chantal says the words: *"avoir le béguin pour quelqu'un."*

"What does that mean?" he asks.

"When you yearn for someone. They're unattainable. But you can't get them out of your mind."

"A crush," Jeremy translates. "So when does a crush become love? When you attain this girl?"

Chantal shakes her head with a sly smile on her face. "One should never attain the object of a crush."

"Why not?"

"You will be disappointed. A crush is about desire. It's not about love."

"But how do you know until you've tried?" Jeremy asks.

The bride and bridegroom lean toward each other and when their lips touch, the photographer snaps a photo and the flower girl giggles.

"I know a place for our picnic," Chantal says.

They walk along the Seine, leaving the photo shoot behind. Jeremy tells her his story.

"One day, toward the end of the summer, a girl came up to me and told me that Sarah liked me. Sarah, the object of my affection. I was out of my mind with excitement. I planned to kiss her that night. I wouldn't talk about it with the other boys in my bunk who boasted about their meager fumblings in the dark—this was love of a higher order. I had waited for weeks, watching her, learning her every stroke. I knew how many twists on her braid, I noticed when a new bathing suit didn't match up with her tan line."

"A romantic," Chantal says.

"A fool," Jeremy tells her.

"We're almost there," Chantal says.

The stone walkway follows the edge of the Seine. Their bags bump against their legs as they walk. Chantal's pace quickens.

This is not the way they usually stroll—slowly, effortlessly, meandering around corners. He lengthens his stride to keep up.

The river is high from days of summer rain. Someone at dinner last night said that there was a threat of flooding, and the conversation turned to Hurricane Katrina. At home, Jeremy had been quick to accuse the Bush administration of doing everything wrong, but here, among Europeans, he is oddly defensive. He found himself arguing that it is impossible to protect a city built below sea level, and he thought to himself, even as the words slipped from his mouth: What am I saying? Do I even believe this?

Later, on the walk home, before the fight, he told Dana, "I'm not sure what that was all about. With these foreigners I find myself rethinking everything I took for granted."

"In Paris, it's still embarrassing to be an American," she said.

"That's not it," Jeremy said. "I mean, I was thinking about it in a brand-new way. What I said made sense to me. I wasn't just making excuses."

She wrapped her arm around his waist and pressed her head into his shoulder. "I'm tired," she said. "Sometimes it's hard to be so sure of myself all the time."

"You?" he said, and kissed the top of her head.

"Especially me," she told him.

The water of the Seine licks the side of this low road. Jeremy doesn't see anything ahead that might provide a spot for a picnic, if that's what Chantal is looking for. Halfway across the river, on the Île Saint-Louis, long stretches of riverbank provide sunbathers a place to stretch out. Jeremy glances at the darkening sky. He imagines the almost naked boys who are lying on the grass at the edge of the island running for cover in a thunderous moment.

But Chantal is not headed for the bridge, which is on the higher road. And Jeremy doesn't ask her plan—that has been one of the delights of his days with Chantal. He gives it all up to her. She leads the way in conversation and in their peregrinations through the city. So why is he feeling anxious all of a sudden? It's not as if they're lost. It's impossible to imagine that they've run out of things to talk about or sights to see.

But there's nothing ahead, just a long stretch of road. They walk, quickly, Chantal's low heels clicking on the cobblestones.

Jeremy remembers the story he was telling—the girl at summer camp—and feels a rush of relief. They are in the middle of a conversation. He can find his way back after all.

"That night, at camp—" he says, but Chantal interrupts him, something she never does.

"Wait a moment," she tells him. "We're almost there. Save your wonderful story."

Jeremy worries—it is not a wonderful story. It is barely a story at all. The girl didn't show up, the other girls teased him, and he avoided the lake for the rest of the summer. Why did he choose to tell this story at all? First love? He could have talked about Dana, because of course, even though there were plenty of girlfriends along the way, she was the first to claim his heart.

"*Nous sommes arrivés,*" Chantal says proudly. Here we are.

She has stopped walking and stands there, her arms open. Jeremy looks around. There is no patch of grass, no tree to sit beneath, nothing that bears noticing.

Until Chantal steps toward the river and then keeps going, down a few steep stairs and onto a short plank. *Une péniche!* She is leading him onto one of the many old boats that are moored along the river. This one in particular is badly in need of painting, though it was once a bold red, with the words JARDIN BLEU painted in yellow on the side. It's not as long as many of the other boats—maybe forty feet—and it looks like it hasn't budged from its spot in years.

Jeremy glances up and down the long stretch of boats and sees immediately what makes this boat different—it is a garden! The deck is covered with potted plants and flowers and ferns, bursting with them, in fact. Flowering tendrils spill over the sides of the boat and hang down, sometimes dropping as low as the water. And a deep, lush jungle smell rushes at him—there's something wild and untamed here.

Chantal is already stepping onto the boat, her long, lean legs easily maneuvering the gap from the quai to the boat. She leans back and gives him a hand. He takes it, though of course he could make this step without her help. The bags on her arm bump against each other and she says, "Let me put these down. Come in. Welcome to my home."

Her home.

He stands with his feet firmly planted on the boat's deck and feels a momentary shift—of course, they're on water—and the boat rolls as a *bateau-mouche* goes by. He catches himself with a hand on the rail. Chantal reaches out her hands and he's confused until he remembers his packages, draped over shoulders and forearms. He unloads them into her hands.

"Please. Take a seat on the deck. I'll be right there." She gestures with a tilt of her head to the back of the boat.

He sees a table and two chairs in the middle of the garden. The table sits under a trellis; wisteria, in full bloom, drapes the wood, cascading down. Jeremy has never seen anything like this before. He must say something, but when he looks back, Chantal is gone. He sees the back of her head as she descends some steps into the belly of the boat.

Again the boat rocks; again Jeremy grabs the rail and widens his stance. I need sea legs, he thinks.

He walks back to the table and chairs, winding through the pots of flowering bushes and exotic ferns. Everything is newly watered from the storm, and the smell of damp earth fills the air.

Chantal's home. Jeremy could have imagined many places where she might have lived—a *chambre de bonne* near the Eiffel Tower, a small apartment on the Left Bank, maybe even a loft in the Marais—but this is beyond his imaginings. And yet it is perfect. That is what it is like to learn someone, he thinks. You know many things about them, and then one new bit of information takes all the knowledge you've gained and shifts it so completely that you begin again.

He walks around the boat, weaving through the planters. Some hold single plants, some hold a wild mixture of foliage that tumbles over the sides of the pots, verdant and alive. There is much color in these plants—shades of purple, from pale to vivid. And the blue! He fills his lungs with a deep breath, taking in the rich, loamy smells.

He hears music—Nina Simone—and he sees the speakers set in the very back of the boat. She is making lunch for him. She has invited him to her home. The boat rides a wave and his hand grabs the rail.

Suddenly he thinks, Will he tell Dana? Of course he will. There's nothing to hide. His French tutor took him for lunch on her houseboat. They sat at a lovely table in the back of the boat and she taught him the words for flowers and plants and river life. He imagines telling this story at a dinner party. Amazing! And your wife bought you the French tutor!

Then he remembers Lindy and her reaction to Chantal. Was

she jealous? Protective of her mother? Worried about losing Jeremy? Impossible. He will assure her that the lessons are over. There was nothing to worry about.

If he even needs to mention it at all.

He hears Chantal making her way up the stairs and he takes his hand off the rail.

"It is wonderful," he tells her as she emerges, carrying a large tray.

She smiles at him, a smile as full as any he has seen. She is home, he thinks. She is where she belongs.

"Our lunch," she says simply.

But it is far from simple. Jeremy follows her to the table, where she sets down the tray. He sees a bottle of red wine and two glasses, a plate of cheese, a basket of bread, a saucer of olives and cornichons, a bowl of sliced apples and pears. Every item of food looks perfect—or perhaps Jeremy is seeing the food as it should be seen, presented almost as a celebration of itself. The plates and bowls are creamy white ceramic, without design, the napkin in the bread basket is a pale rose color.

"A feast," Jeremy says.

He is extraordinarily hungry. He sits at one of the chairs and offers to pour the wine while Chantal sets out the plates.

Then she sits across from him and lifts her glass.

He imagines a toast—last night at dinner there were almost a dozen toasts—to his and Dana's anniversary, to the film, to France, to someone's new book of art criticism, to the great director.

But Chantal simply reaches her glass across the table and clinks it against his. They smile and sip. The wine is delicious.

"Tell me your love story," Chantal says.

"It's nothing," Jeremy says. "I'd like to hear about the boat."

"First, love," Chantal insists.

And so Jeremy begins his story. Or begins again. And this time, his story becomes a fairy tale, an enormous lie. He has never invented stories before.

"That night I went to the canteen at the camp, the place where we all hung out after the evening activity. She was waiting for me. She wore her hair down for the first time and it covered her back like a blanket. I had never seen such beautiful hair."

Chantal looks pleased and so Jeremy continues, his voice deep, the French words spilling from his tongue as if he often sat on a houseboat with a young woman in Paris and fabricated impossible love stories.

"I was shy—I'm still somewhat shy—but then I was often silent in crowds of children, uneasy about myself in ways that made it hard to be free. With Sarah I felt bold, I felt older and wiser and more handsome than I really was."

Chantal laughs and Jeremy takes a sip of the wine.

"Sarah asked me if I liked her. I told her yes. I told her that I thought she was the prettiest girl in the camp. I said that I wished I were old enough to be her boyfriend. She told me that she didn't like the older boys, that they were full of themselves. She liked that I was quiet. So many boys talk about themselves all the time, she said."

Jeremy realized that he was suddenly one of those boys, talking about himself. And none of the story sounded true—it was ludicrous that an older girl would choose such a boy. But Chantal waited for the story to continue, and Jeremy couldn't imagine how to back out of his mistake.

"I asked her if she had ever swum in the lake at night. She

said no, that it wasn't allowed, that she once heard about a girl who went for a night swim and never came back. 'Let's go,' I said. 'It's safe. No one will find us.' "

"Brave boy," Chantal says.

No, Jeremy wants to shout. *I am not that brave boy! I have never been that brave boy.*

"We walked down to the lakeshore. There was a dance that night, so everyone was in the dance hall or the canteen—there was no one else at the beach. And it was so dark we could barely see each other. This is deep in the countryside of New Hampshire, far from any city lights or noise."

"Sounds lovely," Chantal says. She closes her eyes at one point, and Jeremy imagines that she is at the lake with him, standing at the water's edge, conjuring up the nerve to take off her clothes.

"I was the first to undress. We walked out to the edge of the dock and I left my clothes in a bundle on the wood planks and then dove in a nervous rush into the water. When I came up for air she was mid-dive, naked, incredibly beautiful. I had never seen a naked girl before."

Jeremy stops talking. He hasn't eaten and somehow his first glass of wine is gone. He has had nothing to eat today but a few scraps of bread with olive oil. Maybe it's the slow roll of the boat, but he feels off balance.

"Let the naked girl stop mid-dive," he says, "but I need some of this cheese."

Chantal laughs. "Poor Sarah," she says. "Exposed like that."

"Sarah can wait for the cool splash of the water. I can no longer wait."

He reaches for some bread and slices into the Camembert

that has run onto the plate. He spreads it onto the bread and fills his mouth with its pungent taste. Chantal takes a slice of pear, a slice of chèvre, lays one on top of the other, and passes it to him.

"*Merci,*" he says. The food seems to dissolve in his mouth.

"Please," he says. "Tell me your story of first love so I can eat instead of talking."

"But this is a French lesson," Chantal says, smiling at him. She seems to be teasing him, but he's not sure how. "You are supposed to talk."

"Challenge my French with your story. Tell me a very complicated love story."

"When you are done," Chantal says.

For four days Jeremy has wished he could charm Chantal with stories, but he is not that sort of man. He is a listener, something that always made women respond to him as if he were better than the rest of his species. And now? He's worse than the worst of them. He's lying. And he can't stop himself.

"She dove in a perfect arc, the moonlight revealing enough of her long, slim body for me to see her small breasts, her slim hips. And then she was in the water and racing toward me. I was treading water, caught in my Peeping Tom stare, and I thought she would swim right at me and pull me under. But she swam past me and kept swimming. I had to chase her and so I did, though of course she was faster and stronger than I."

The boat wobbles and Jeremy grasps the table. Chantal laughs.

"The *bateau-mouche,*" she explains. "Even in the middle of the night I find myself thinking I'll tumble from my bed and drown."

For the first time, Jeremy considers that below deck is Chantal's home. There will be a bed in the room. He looks away from her and out toward the river. On the deck of the *bateau-mouche* tourists wave at them, insistently. And foolishly, Jeremy waves back.

They think I'm French, he thinks.

But of course Chantal is not waving. How silly, he thinks. If you live here, you would never wave back.

I'm behaving like a thirteen-year-old boy, Jeremy thinks.

"You are swimming for dear life," Chantal says.

End the story, Jeremy says to himself. Now.

"I would never have caught her. She was much too strong. So she must have slowed down for me, kind girl that she was. And when I caught her, somewhere out in the middle of the lake, I didn't know what to do with her. I was so young. And she was beyond me in every way."

"She showed you," Chantal said.

"Yes," Jeremy agreed. "She showed me what to do."

They sip their wine. This time Jeremy prepares an apple slice and a piece of Roquefort for Chantal, who takes it gladly and eats it with pleasure. He refills their wine.

He feels an odd combination of relief—his story is over—and horror, as he is a man who invents himself to impress a young woman. At forty-five! Only a week ago, while lying in their bed in the Santa Monica Canyon, he had traced his fingers over Dana's body and said, "I know every inch of you."

"No surprises?" she had asked. "No chance to discover a scar on my leg, a tattoo on my hip?"

"I don't want surprises," he had said, pulling her closer. "I want just what we have. Nothing more."

Dana hadn't said anything. And for a quick, uncertain moment, Jeremy had thought, Maybe she wants more. She's a woman of big emotions, a woman who lives life on a grand scale. And then she comes home to me. He felt an ache in his chest. *Talk about it,* he thought. But as so often happened, words didn't come—they jammed up against one another somewhere inside him. He did what he knew how to do. He took Dana in his arms and made love to her, covering her small body with his own.

When they were done, he wrapped his arm around her familiar body and pressed himself against her back. Now he wonders: Was last night's argument a way of twisting around his own fears? Is this part of his unease these last days in Paris? After ten years of loving Dana, has he lost his faith in their relationship?

"Tell me the story of your first love," he says to Chantal, pushing his thoughts away.

She looks toward the river for a moment and seems almost shy again. Then she busies herself with the cheese and the pears.

"Or tell me the names of all the plants in your garden," Jeremy says quickly.

"You're kind," she says. "An escape is offered."

"If you'd like. I can't even remember how we got to the dangerous topic of love."

"My fault," Chantal says, smiling. "The head of the language school would fire me."

Jeremy smiles. "I won't tell." He wonders if lunch on her houseboat would also be *interdit*. Of course. The thought pleases him. She's breaking the rules for him.

"I fell in love for the first time a year ago," she says. She stops as if that is the end of her story.

"No stormy adolescent romances?" Jeremy asks.

"Plenty of storms. No calm after the storm."

Jeremy nods. Yes. He knows what she means. He loved falling in love with Dana, but then, to his great surprise, he found that he enjoyed being in love with her even more. The calm.

And now? Is he creating a storm out of thin air?

"I met Philippe at the language school. Every spring there is a party to celebrate the director's birthday. It's a silly thing—the director is like a child in many ways. He would like all of us to teach our classes with games and prizes and songs. I'm not very good at that and so he uses me for the private lessons."

Jeremy cannot imagine Chantal in front of a class of adults, singing a French ditty and tossing bonbons to the best student. And of course, he can't imagine himself in such a class. How lucky, he thinks, that we found each other.

"Philippe was new to the school. He is very handsome—I am not usually drawn to men like him."

Men like him. Jeremy has always been told that he is handsome. But because he is shy, or quiet, or less bold than most good-looking men, he has always felt that he has little in common with a ladies' man, a Romeo.

"He spoke to me at the end of the party. I had been watching him, of course—every woman had her eyes on Philippe. And then his eyes were on me. He has that ability to make you feel that you're the only one."

She stops and her gaze drifts off—she follows the passing of a tugboat along the river. She looks sad, as if this isn't a love story at all.

"I'm sorry," she says, looking back at him. "Perhaps I shouldn't have started this."

"Go on," Jeremy says.

"Enough new vocabulary," she tells him. "It's our last day together."

She reaches for the wine and refills their glasses. Her story continues with a surer voice now.

"We left the party and went to a café, had another drink together. He's a charming man, of course—he knows how to win a woman's heart. And I suppose I was waiting to give mine away. Twenty-eight years old. I'm a little out of step with my generation."

"Except for the hippie commune in the Indian Ocean," Jeremy says.

"Oh, that. An aberration. A desperate attempt to be youthful and wild."

"Look at you here," Jeremy says. "This is wild." He opens his arms to the jardin she has created on the Seine.

"This is just my refuge."

"From what?"

"From the busyness of the world. I come here to hide."

Jeremy thinks of himself in his workshop. He is happiest there, whether he is working on a project for a client or building a new armoire for their home. He likes the smell of sawdust, the sound of a plane trueing the edge of a plank, the steady focus of design. When Dana goes to work she is surrounded by people and words and passions so large that they move others to tears. So what happens at the end of the day? Does she really want what he offers? Why is he suddenly worried about this, after so many years of confident love?

"Philippe and I dated for a while and I enjoyed his attention. He's a funny man—I think he truly believes he falls in love with every woman he dates. In fact, I think he's merely in love with love. It fills him up for a while, makes him think life is grand. And it *is* grand. He's very good at love."

"But you—you said you fell in love."

"One weekend we went to visit his parents in the Loire. They have a weekend home near a grand château, one of those the tourists like to visit. This one offers classical concerts in the summer. They're lovely, really. Everyone sits on the great lawn under a canopy of stars and the air fills with the music of some wonderful symphony.

"Philippe took me to one of these concerts. We brought a picnic—not unlike the one we have here."

Jeremy feels a pang of proprietary jealousy, as if this might be the only time Chantal had offered such a display of food. *Idiot*, he thinks.

"We ate and drank and listened to the music. At one point, in the middle of the concert, Philippe took my hand and gestured for me to follow him. We made our way through the crowds of people while the orchestra played. I started to ask him where we were going, but he put his finger to his lips. He looked positively delighted with himself, so I let him lead me away.

"We circled behind the château. The building was closed and only the dramatic outdoor lighting was in use—illuminating the turrets, the massive entrance, the balconies, the guard towers on each end. No one lives in the château anymore. It is used for tours and is rented out for weddings and business functions. Perhaps someone lives in the caretaker's cottage at the entrance, but this evening there was no sign of anyone patrolling the place.

"Philippe knew of a door in the back—a part of the servants' quarters—that had a broken padlock. I wondered if he had taken other women here before me, but I pushed the thought away. We sneaked into the château and climbed the many stairs to the master bedroom, guided by Philippe's flashlight. We stepped over the rope that blocked the entrance to the room and Philippe took me to bed."

Chantal is looking at her hands, which rest on the table in front of her. She has long, tapered fingers and pale skin. Jeremy imagines those hands on his face. And then Chantal looks at him, breaking her own trance. Her eyes are bright and wide.

"I had never done anything so daring in my life. I loved him that night."

She stops speaking and shakes her head.

"Crazy. Imagine if we were caught."

"Did you love him or did you love danger?" Jeremy asks.

Chantal looks puzzled.

"I'm sorry," Jeremy says quickly. "It's none of my business."

"It's a good question," Chantal says. "I can answer it." She pauses and sips her wine. "I loved him."

"And you still love him?"

"I don't know," Chantal says.

"Does he make you a more daring person?" Jeremy asks.

"For one night," Chantal says with a sly smile. "And for that I loved him."

Jeremy doesn't understand. He wants to ask questions but he feels that he has intruded enough.

And then, like a sudden storm, he feels irrationally angry: What does breaking into a château and making love in someone else's bed have to do with love?

For a moment he confuses Chantal with his daughter. He wants to give her advice, tell her that she's wrong, that Philippe is the wrong man, that love has nothing to do with danger. And then a loudspeaker breaks their uneasy silence and he hears a static-filled roar of words—something about Notre Dame and the Île Saint-Louis. It is the *bateau-mouche* again. And again, tourists are waving madly. Why? What would it matter if he waved back? He turns away from them and reaches for more cheese.

She places her hand on his. "I'm sorry," she says. "It was an inappropriate story."

"I remember what you said at the café earlier," Jeremy says. "That sometimes we have to run away from ourselves to find ourselves. Maybe Philippe helped you do that."

Chantal smiles. "I like that. And so I have learned once again that I am truly a good girl at heart. And I should find myself a better man."

He looks at her hand and she takes it away.

Jeremy is not accustomed to so much talk. If he were younger, he would take her hand and lead her downstairs to her bedroom. No, it has nothing to do with age. He would do it now. This is the moment he has waited for since he arrived at the métro this morning.

He thinks about sex with Dana. In bed with her, he finds his truest self. Their lovemaking is deep and rich—they rarely speak in bed, and yet he feels he knows her best when they've made love. She gives herself to him, he gives himself to her. In ten years, their passion has not quieted.

"Let's walk," he says to Chantal.

She stands too quickly and knocks the table. Her glass of wine topples and Jeremy catches it before it falls to the deck. But wine spills on Chantal's sandaled feet.

"Oh, how clumsy!" she says, and her face turns the same shade of pink as her blouse. She flees—Jeremy can hear her feet clattering down the stairs of the boat and into the space below.

Jeremy cleans up. Most of the wine landed on her feet, and he mops what landed on the deck with a napkin dipped in water.

He gathers the bowls and plates and basket and puts them back on the tray. Much of the food is gone—and so is the wine. He's surprised to see the empty bottle.

He'd clear the dishes, but he knows that the kitchen is below—along with Chantal and her bedroom. No, he'll leave it all here.

His cell phone rings. He pulls it out of his back pocket. It is Dana.

For a moment he feels caught—but then he shakes his head. *I've done nothing wrong. A lunch, some wine.*

"*Allô?*" He says it with a French accent—she'll be amused, he thinks.

"I'm sorry," she says quickly, and then in French: "I have the wrong number."

She hangs up before he can stop her.

He calls her back.

"It was me," he says in English. "I was pretending to be your dashing French lover." And then Chantal is standing there, in front of him. He looks down. She is wearing white sneakers—Keds—and again he thinks of his daughter.

Dana laughs, her movie laugh—rich and deep. Chantal takes the tray and walks away.

"I'd like to meet her," Dana says.

"Who?"

"The French tutor."

"Why?"

"Lindy says she is very pretty."

"You saw Lindy?"

"Not yet. She called. Bring your tutor to meet me."

"The lesson is almost over," Jeremy says, though it's not. He glances at his watch. Two P.M. "There's no reason to meet her." He lowers his voice to a whisper.

"We're shooting early. Pascale called a couple of hours ago. Something about the rain. She's setting up now. I want you both to come."

"Where?"

"The Pont des Arts. Your little friend will enjoy it."

"Dana."

"Lindy says you're smitten."

"She didn't say that. That's not even a word she would know."

"Maybe we're all taking language lessons these days."

"Dana."

"I've got to go, sweetheart. Come by soon. We start in half an hour."

"Where's Lindy—"

"She'll be there."

"Did she tell you about the monastery?"

"Monastery? I have to throw clothes on and dash over there. I'll see you soon."

She hangs up.

Chantal is gone. So is the food, the wine, the momentary illusion of a different Jeremy.

No, he thinks. He will not bring her to meet Dana. Lindy was behaving like a petulant child. That's all.

He remembers Chantal's hand on his.

He thinks of his house in the Santa Monica Canyon, his dog, his shop, and he wishes he were home.

He walks to the front of the boat. He sees the stairs—a steep

ladder really—that lead below. He can't hear anything—no
dishes being washed, no water running.

"Chantal?" he calls.

"*J'arrive,*" she says. I'm coming.

She appears at the bottom of the ladder and looks up at him.
Has she been crying? Did he say something on the phone that
would have upset her? *There's no reason to meet her.*

He steps back and lets her pass by. She keeps on walking and
he follows her to the edge of the boat and then onto the quai.
This time she does not offer her hand as he leaps from the boat
to the land.

"My wife invited us—" he begins and she turns to him. She
has put on lipstick. Her lips are moist. I can go back, he thinks. I
can take her hand.

"Yes?"

"—to watch them film. She thought you might be interested."

"How nice of her."

"We don't have to."

"Of course," Chantal says.

"It's very slow. It's nothing as glamorous as Hollywood
would like us to believe."

"I'd like that very much."

Lindy meets them at the entrance to the Pont des Arts. A huge
crowd has gathered behind barricades on both sides of the river.
Lindy hands them badges on twine that they hang around their
necks.

"*Mon papa!*" she tells the young guard, who has not taken his
eyes off the girl. Jeremy looks at his daughter through this man's
eyes. She is luminous, despite the shaved head—the word "ripe"

comes to mind, and Jeremy hates himself for the thought of it. She's wearing a tight tank top over breasts that seem to have grown since last fall. She's gained a little weight, which becomes her—her face is fuller, her body less waiflike. Jeremy looks back at the guard and wants to deck him.

Lindy leads them through the opening in the barricade and past the guard. She takes Jeremy's hand as if she were a child. His heart swells. She is still his child, he thinks.

He feels the tug back to his life, this daughter he never imagined he'd have, ten years of girldom, a complicated path through the teenage wilderness and now this, a quest to a monastery and back. All his. He squeezes her hand.

Ahead, in the middle of the bridge, is a whirlwind of noise and commotion and equipment and lights—in the center of it all a petite, wild-haired redhead, Pascale, shouts commands. Jeremy likes Pascale. She's a director Dana has worked with before, and she seems to keep her sanity in this crazy business. Pascale catches his eye and blows a kiss. She points toward a tent at the other end of the bridge. And then she goes back to yelling at a couple of ponytailed guys carrying a bed. A bed on the bridge?

"Did you meet your friends?" Jeremy asks Lindy as they walk toward the tent.

"No friends," she says. "I was leaving you to your French lesson." She glances back at Chantal, who follows a step or two behind. "Why is she here?"

"Your mother invited her," Jeremy says quietly, hoping Chantal cannot hear.

Jeremy looks back at Chantal. She is distracted by the set and the crowd—her eyes are wide, her face aglow. She moves up closer to them.

"*Maman!*" Lindy calls.

Dana is standing at the entrance to the tent, watching them. Jeremy, caught between Chantal and Lindy, in the middle of the thick crowd, feels Chantal's arm against his. He can't move away. Dana smiles as if she knows what he's thinking.

She's a mess, his beautiful wife. She wears no makeup—or is she wearing makeup to distort her perfect features? Her tan skin is pale, her hair flat and dull, her clothes baggy and worn. Is this a costume?

For an impossible moment, Jeremy thinks she's someone else—his wife's ugly assistant—and in a moment the star will emerge from her tent.

But Dana steps toward him and kisses his lips. Then she extends a hand toward Chantal.

"*Enchantée,*" she says, her voice that buttery movie voice that everyone loves. At night, Jeremy hears a different voice: her bed voice, he calls it. He thinks of it as a voice she saves for him, unlike the voice she shares with the world.

"So pleased to meet you," Chantal says. "I've heard so much about you."

Lies, Jeremy thinks. He has invented a gorgeous wife, a glamorous wife, a larger-than-life wife. He has invented himself today as well. A boy who dives into a summer lake with a naked girl. A man who seduces a woman on a houseboat on the Seine.

What if everything you've always been sure of—your wife's beauty, your own fidelity—gets shaken?

"You look awful!" Lindy says.

Dana rubs her hand over Lindy's head and then pulls her daughter to her and embraces her. It is a powerful hug; the girl is engulfed in her mother's arms.

"What's this?" Dana asks, pulling back and peering at Lindy's scalp.

"It will grow back," Lindy says.

"You look gorgeous," Dana tells her.

"Really?" Lindy says, truly surprised.

"Really."

Lindy throws her arms around her mother. Over Lindy's shoulder Dana rolls her eyes, her smile broad and happy.

"Is this your costume?" Lindy asks. "What are you?"

Dana laughs. "I'm a wreck, apparently. I've just lost my husband to a younger woman." She glances at Chantal. "And I've been caught in a rainstorm. We're hoping it rains again. Though I can't imagine looking any worse than this."

Her role, Jeremy thinks, and he feels his shoulders relax, his chest expand. Of course. It *is* makeup—he can see now that new lines have been etched into his wife's flawless skin.

He can't remember the story of this film, though he's sure that she's told him. Have I not been paying attention? he thinks. But that's who he is—a man who listens. When did she tell me the story? Last night at dinner? Months ago when she got the script? Why have I forgotten?

"Why is there a bed on the bridge?" he asks in French.

"See," Dana says. "I knew you spoke French beautifully. Never with me, though." She turns to Chantal. "I talk too much. See what happens if I stop talking?"

"I've been making mistakes all day," Jeremy says. It is another mistake. Suddenly everything has two meanings. Jeremy feels off balance.

"*Le lit?*" he repeats.

"Ah, the bed," Dana says.

"*Attention! Atten-ci-on!*" Pascale shouts over the loudspeaker. The movie is a French and American collaboration. The cast is half French, half American. Even the dialogue is a jumble of both languages. Jeremy remembers that much.

"I must go," Dana says, while Pascale shouts something over the loudspeaker. "I'm on right away. I hope we can talk later." She says this last to Chantal, who seems inordinately pleased to receive the attentions of this actress, even if she is homely, poorly dressed, and the wife of the man who has spent the day pining for her.

I mean nothing to her, Jeremy thinks, and then he catches himself. Of course not. I'm this week's student. On Monday she'll meet another student.

Dana hurries off.

"Come on," Lindy says, breathlessly. "I want to be in front."

She sounds like a little girl at her first shoot. She should know better—that it will take longer than they anticipate to set up the scene, that something will go wrong right away and they'll have to find a new lens or bring in the jib or reset the lighting. And if it does rain, they'll need tarps above the cameramen and director, even while the actors get soaked.

Lindy dashes ahead through the crowd.

"Are you sure—" Jeremy says. He wants Chantal to say, *Let's leave. Let's go someplace quiet.*

"Oh, I can't wait to see them film!" she says. Of course, she is starstruck. Everyone is. Except for him. Can he love his wife and hate the star?

Jeremy takes Chantal's elbow and they maneuver through the crowd. Pascale has cleared a large space in the middle of the bridge. The bed sits there, with a single rose-colored sheet covering it. No blanket, no pillows. The sheet is rumpled as if already used.

The sky darkens and thunder rumbles—the crowd lets out a collective *Ooooh!* They are waiting for drama and the approaching storm feeds their expectation. Nothing is happening yet on the set, but onlookers have quieted. Jeremy sees that gawkers on both sides of the Seine, lined up three or four deep, are obediently following the demands of the signs that have been lifted by young crew members. *Silence!*

Jeremy finds Lindy at the front edge of the set and he helps Chantal squeeze in beside her. He then fits himself in the space between them. He knows only a few of the film people who hover near Pascale—he recognizes them from the last film Dana made with her, four years before. One of them was at dinner last night—a young Frenchman who worked with Pascale on the script. "He's brilliant," Dana told Jeremy while the young man told a long story about the immigrant revolution brewing in the *banlieue* of Paris. And pompous, Jeremy thought, but he didn't say a word. Now the young man fixes Dana's oversize shirt, unbuttoning two of the top buttons. He's not from the costume department, Jeremy thinks. What business is it of his? But Pascale looks over and nods—apparently Dana should look horrible and bare her breasts at the same time.

Pascale calls out some commands and then takes her seat on her director's chair. The chair reads BIG BOSS. It was a gift from an earlier crew and Pascale uses it for every film now. It is the "big" part that Pascale likes. She is barely five feet tall.

Again, the sky grumbles and Pascale claps and raises her hands to the heavens. A few people laugh.

And then they are ready to film the scene. Jeremy wonders

how it has happened so quickly, but perhaps things have changed since the last time he watched a shoot. We'll watch a scene or two and then move on, he thinks.

There is quiet and then a man and a woman walk onto the set. They are wearing bathrobes. They take off the robes and hand them to a young woman at their side. They are naked. There is a muffled gasp from the crowd. Pascale raises a hand and everyone quiets. A woman smacks the clapper board and the cameras roll.

Jeremy glances at Chantal—she is transfixed. And then Lindy—her mouth has fallen open. Jeremy wants to cover her eyes. But of course, she's twenty, she's seen naked boys before. Men.

Chantal shifts her weight and he feels the pressure of her arm on his. She doesn't move away.

The woman is very young, barely older than Lindy. She's blond and her skin is ghostly white—she looks like some cross between angel and child prostitute. Her body is impossibly perfect—small and curvaceous with breasts as round as apples. Jeremy sees that her pubic hair is shaved! No wonder she looks like a child. There's something unsettling about what she offers—sex and innocence—something pornographic, he thinks.

She walks to the bed and lies down. She doesn't seem to have any self-consciousness about her nudity. Jeremy wonders about children along the quai watching this. But we're in Paris, he thinks. And for a moment, he wonders what kind of rating this movie might have. Of course, Dana has never done an X-rated film—it would kill her career. She's a classy actress, like a younger Meryl Streep with a little more sass. She has never even done a sex scene in the nude.

Will someone cover the girl's bare crotch?

The man walks around the bed, looking at the girl. He, too, is comfortable with his naked body. He has a large uncircumcised penis that weaves as he walks. Jeremy's body tenses. He shouldn't be here with these two girls at his side. Dana should not have invited them. He feels like a prude—this shouldn't even be a public event.

He looks up. A camera moves in close. Dana is hidden from sight. No one has spoken a word.

The man is older than the girl, by a good twenty years. In fact, his body is a little slack—Jeremy sees with wicked pleasure that the man has a bit of extra weight around his waist. But it doesn't concern him; he's circling the bed and the naked girl as if he's a lion tamer. Or the lion himself. The girl is his prey.

Dana steps forward. Someone has poured water on her and she's dripping wet. Her clothes cling to her; beads of water drip from her chin. This is no summer rainstorm—it looks as if she's stepped from the shower. Jeremy expects Pascale to stop the filming, to yell at the person responsible for overdoing the effect this way—but the camera keeps moving, Dana keeps walking toward the man, and the man keeps circling the girl on the bed.

"Look at me," Dana says, her voice a throaty whisper.

The man doesn't look. He walks by her and keeps walking. The girl on the bed makes a moaning sound as if she's already having sex. Jeremy is disgusted. What is this? The girl follows the man's eyes with her own—her pleasure comes from his attention. She's aroused; even her nipples stand out from her perky breasts. How did she do that? Can a woman make her nipples erect as part of her acting training? She can't possibly be aroused by this fool with the big dick, Jeremy thinks.

"*Regarde,*" Dana says, her voice more insistent.

Thunder, right on cue. Was that real? Everyone looks up—

except for the actors, who ignore the low rumble and the first drops of rain.

A few of the technicians look at Pascale, who gestures with her hand: *Keep going, keep going.*

The man sits on the edge of the bed. The girl curls toward him. Dana stops and watches them. Her face shows confusion, then pain.

The man takes the girl in his arms and lies down next to her. It seems as if the girl is a half second from orgasm already. Her body is writhing, her low moan is rising. Jeremy thinks she should be pulled from the movie—she is overacting. She belongs in a porn film, not in a serious film of Dana's!

The man strokes the girl's body, petting her as if she is, in fact, his cat. She purrs. *Oh, God, stop!* Jeremy wants to scream. *What is this?*

Then Dana circles the bed, watching them. Her expression changes—is she enjoying this? Jeremy hopes that someone will let him in on the joke. Has Pascale made her first comedy?

Dana sits at the edge of the bed. She reaches out her hand and lets it rest on the man's hip. He's facing away from her, covering the girl with his caresses. He doesn't seem to notice Dana.

It's a fantasy, Jeremy decides. The bed, the naked lovers, the distraught woman. She's imagining this. And in a rare moment of poor cinematic taste, Pascale has brought the fantasy to life. On a bridge in the middle of the Seine.

Spare me, Jeremy thinks.

He turns to Chantal. He'll shake his head, show her his disgust. But she doesn't take her eyes from the scene in front of her.

The rain gathers force. No one moves. A red umbrella ap-

pears above Pascale's head. The crowd along the Seine leans forward over the barricades and peers—what can they see? Jeremy
wonders. Do they see the man's cock, the girl's shaved vagina?
Do they see Dana's look of desire? What does she desire? The
man? The girl? He wants to scream "*Arrête!*"

And then—thank God!—Pascale yells, "Cut!" and calls,
"Bravo!" The crowd applauds, as if they were at the ballet and
the performance was exquisite. Jeremy can't imagine what
everyone is so goddamn pleased about. He's the only one not
cheering.

"It's art," Chantal says, almost breathlessly.

"What?" Jeremy barks.

Chantal looks at him, surprised.

"That was beautiful. She has the most expressive face."

Jeremy feels like a prude. Maybe everyone was looking at his
wife's face when all he could see was a penis and a vagina.

Dana walks over to them, grabs Jeremy's arm, and calls, "Follow me!"

She wraps one hand around Jeremy's elbow and the other
around Chantal's arm. She maneuvers them toward her tent at
the far end of the bridge. Only then does Jeremy realize that the
skies have opened and the rain is pounding on them.

"Lindy!" he shouts. He feels a sudden panic, as if she has disappeared in the middle of this chaos.

"I'll be there in a minute!" Lindy calls back.

Jeremy turns—she is right behind them and then she turns
toward a young man with a clipboard and begins talking to him
in French.

"Let's get out of all this!" Dana shouts.

"All this" is the storm, the relentless grumble of thunder, the clatter of rain on the iron bridge, the movie people herding equipment in every direction. And Pascale is braying over the loudspeaker. Jeremy can't understand a word she says.

Dana's assistant opens the flap of the tent as if she's been waiting all day to save her boss from the rain, and Dana shouts, "You're a love!" as they rush through—first Dana, then Chantal, then Jeremy. The assistant follows them and leads Dana behind a screen, where she helps her out of her wet clothes. Jeremy knows the young woman—she's been with Dana for a couple of years now. He likes her more than most, because this is all she wants—not her boss's job, just this: to make her boss's job a little easier. She's a simple girl, and there aren't many of those in the movie industry.

"Don't say a word," Dana says from behind the screen. "I know what you're thinking. I know you're horrified."

"You're horrified?" Chantal asks Jeremy.

"He's horrified. I warned him. But still—I wanted you to come. Wait. Let me dry my hair. Go on, Elizabeth. Would you get them hot tea? I can do the rest."

Elizabeth emerges from behind the screen. She hurries to a makeshift kitchen: hot pot, small fridge, all set up for a few hours' shoot on a bridge in the middle of the Seine. Jeremy is still amazed by what the film industry can pull off—not only on the screen, but for the working lives of its stars.

"Is it the nudity?" Chantal asks Jeremy quietly. Does she not want Dana to hear? No, she is encouraging me to speak, Jeremy thinks. She knows that in a moment Dana might answer for me.

And oddly, he wishes Dana would answer for him. He doesn't quite know why he's so upset. It's not the nudity—it's the absurdity of the scene. It's something else: It's Dana.

"You would not do that," Jeremy says to Dana as she steps

from behind the screen, wrapped in a plush robe, a towel turban around her wet hair.

"What would I not do?" Dana asks.

"You would not sit there and watch them."

"You don't know my character," she says simply.

"No one would watch them."

"It's a fantasy."

"But it's a playing-out of someone's inner desires. To watch her husband and his lover? That's absurd."

"What would I do?" Dana asks.

"I don't know," Jeremy says quickly. "I guess—you're right—I don't know your character in this film."

"What is she like, the role you play?" Chantal asks. She leans forward, eagerly taking it all in. For a moment, Jeremy had forgotten about her. They have switched to English. Chantal speaks perfect English! She has an American accent! Again, everything shifts in the kaleidoscope that is this young woman. I know nothing about her, Jeremy realizes. And I thought I— he stops his own thought. What did he think? That he wanted to sleep with her? That he wanted to love her? It seems ridiculous to him now. He's as foolish as the man swinging his dick on the set.

Dana takes a teacup from her assistant and sips at it. "I play a wealthy American woman who has come to Paris with her husband. She shops while the husband has his business meetings. But at some point during the day she finds him strolling through the park with a young girl—"

"Who wrote this film?" Jeremy asks, interrupting her. His heartbeat is fast, his palms are damp. It's clammy in this tent and the rain beats heavily on the canvas, creating a kind of hum like a beehive nearby.

"Claude," Dana says. "The young man you met at dinner."

"He's a kid," Jeremy snorts.

"A very bright kid."

"What does he know about love?"

"You're so funny, darling," Dana says.

Jeremy looks at her, surprised.

She is smiling at him, her wide, gracious smile. She reaches out and touches his arm. "Not everyone knows love like we do."

Jeremy is lost. He can't find any words—in any language. His mind churns and comes up with nothing.

And then the flap of the tent flies open and Lindy dashes in, laughing.

"Oh my God, that was wild! Wild! How did that happen? I mean, the storm in the middle of the scene! It was like you planned it that way." She shakes her body like a wet dog and water flies everywhere. She is radiant—the shine of her scalp seems to light up her face.

"And that girl on the bed," Jeremy says. "That was pornography."

"You're still here," Lindy says, staring at Chantal.

"Lindy—" Jeremy says.

Chantal stands. "I must go."

"No," Dana says. "She's being rude. You're my guest now. Please stay."

Chantal looks at Jeremy. He nods. "No reason to leave," he says weakly.

Chantal looks at her watch. "The lesson is over anyway. And I will be meeting two other tutors."

"How do you speak English so well?" Jeremy asks.

"It is a long story," Chantal says.

"I bet she had an American boyfriend," Lindy says. "That's the way to learn a language. In bed."

Chantal smiles and her face flushes.

"I will walk you out," Jeremy says.

"No need—"

"Please," he insists.

She nods. She turns back to Dana. "It was a pleasure to meet you," she says in French. "Thank you for the opportunity to watch you work."

Dana steps toward her. She kisses Chantal on both cheeks.

"You are a lovely girl," she says. "I'm glad my husband had a chance to spend his week with you."

Again, Chantal's cheeks flush. She turns to Lindy. *"Au revoir et bonne chance."*

"Why do I need luck?" Lindy asks.

Chantal just smiles.

She walks out of the tent and Jeremy follows.

The rain has stopped and the bridge is in the process of a remarkable transformation. A group of young men in black T-shirts that read BOSS'S BOYS shovel sand on the wooden deck of the bridge. The bed is gone and someone has moved a palm tree into its place.

"Pascale has lost her mind," Jeremy mutters.

Chantal laughs.

"This is like magic," she says.

"I guess it is," Jeremy says with a smile. "I'm a little too serious."

"I like that," Chantal says.

They are speaking French again—it is the language they have shared all week and Jeremy finds it hard to speak to her in English. He wishes she didn't speak English at all; somehow that has changed things between them. If he gets stuck, he could have an out. But he didn't know that all week. He just kept pushing on, into unfamiliar territory.

"You didn't really need French lessons, you know," Chantal says. "Your French is excellent."

"But I needed you to guide me along the way," Jeremy says as they walk away from the set and toward the Louvre on the Right Bank. "In French. And in Paris."

"Sometimes I forgot that it was a language lesson," Chantal says.

"Yes," Jeremy tells her. "It felt more like—" He can't think of a word, in either language.

Chantal glances at him, waiting.

"Thank you," he says.

He has stopped at the end of the bridge. She will pass through the barricade and return to Paris; he will turn back and return to the wild world of his wife and his daughter and a bed on the bridge in the middle of the Seine.

He kisses Chantal on both cheeks. She presses her hand on his arm as he does so.

And then she turns and walks toward the crowd, who are waiting for the next scene.

He watches Chantal disappear into the throngs of people. Then he turns back. He thinks about later tonight, when he will be in bed with Dana—it doesn't matter what bed in what country. He will wrap himself around his wife. He will be able to say what he wants to say to her, without words.

The Tutors

quatorze ans dé[...]

à Paris et que vou[...]

Si souvent à votre

[...]ière ; Germaine est

aujourd'hui, qu'el[...]

[...]en petite alors,

[...] cependant, rép[...]

dan Vauvenin, a[...]

[...]alité appréciable

[...]te prie combien

intéressants à son

[...]nous formons pa[...]

*C*hantal is the first to arrive at La Forêt, but she's not surprised. She's always on time, which means that she's always waiting for everyone else to arrive. She's glad to have a moment to herself, to drink a glass of wine, to watch the others as they enter.

The café is at the end of an alley in the Marais. In the summer the tables spill into the street. She got a table under the awning just in case the rain returns. She hears music, but can't see the street musicians—they're blocked by a group of tourists, who watch as their guide points out a small synagogue tucked between two old buildings on the side of the street. The guide's loud voice—Italian—fights to be heard over the chanteuse. Chantal imagines that yet another African American jazz singer has come to Paris to find success. The voice is throaty and deep, and the sound is ragged yet haunting. The walking tour moves on, and now Chantal can see the musicians—a very young white girl sings, accompanied by her father on guitar. The girl must be eleven or twelve, skinny and knock-kneed, timid behind the mike. How can that little thing produce such a big, mournful sound? How does she know enough about life to give the words weight?

Chantal closes her eyes and imagines a different singer— a tall, willowy black woman with closely cropped hair, wide oval eyes, a look of tragedy about her. And, as she takes in the song—a Cole Porter song about the pain of saying goodbye— she thinks about Jeremy. The minute he saw his wife on the bridge, something about him changed. She could see it in his face—he had come home to his wife. He might have spent a day flirting with romance, with the possibility of love, but he belonged to someone else.

She does not belong to Philippe.

She remembers their first date. He invited her to stroll around the Parc des Buttes Chaumont, where she had never been. Mid-tour, Philippe recited a poem by François Villon about the Montfaucon gallows on the western edge of the park. She had kissed him then, stirred by the poetry, his Mick Jagger mouth, and the surprise of those lush hills in the middle of the nineteenth arrondissement. Months later one of his bandmates had teased her: Did she fall for the first-date trick? And then she remembered the waiter at the café near the park who somehow knew Philippe's name. So—he brought all his first dates there.

Philippe loves falling in love, she reminds herself. He does not love being in love.

This day began with Philippe kissing another woman. And where will it end?

She hopes that it's Nico who arrives first. She thinks about their one night in bed, a drunken jaunt that turned into something else the moment he touched her. She closes her eyes and remembers this: They had finished making love and she turned toward him in the narrow bed. He tangled his fingers in her hair.

"Thank you," he whispered. "For this one night."

For a moment she thought: What would it be like to be loved by this man.

When she opens her eyes, she sees the skinny white kid singing the blues.

She wants *something* tonight. She doesn't know what it is—maybe just a yearning for the day not to end.

She looks up as someone walks by her table—not Nico, not Philippe. It's a young girl who looks lost, scanning the tables for *Maman* or *Papa*. The girl turns and dashes down the street. Chantal thinks of Lindy, back with Dana and Jeremy, no longer lost, at least for a little while.

She watches a couple at the table beside her. The woman is telling a long story, her hands waving wildly in the air, and the man, handsome and bored, glances in her direction. She realizes with sudden clarity that Philippe will not show up tonight. Perhaps he finally lured his big-breasted American into bed. Or he'll take the new singer in the band to the Buttes Chaumont and recite a poem to her.

She knows what he won't tell any of his friends or lovers: He lost his brother in a car accident a year ago. The brother had been the good son, the med student, the one who showed up at his parents' *grand appartement* in the sixteenth arrondissement every Sunday for lunch. Philippe had dropped out of school and used up all his money on drugs and music equipment. When he had gone to his family for help, they had cut him off.

He told Chantal all of this late one night after he came back from his parents' place. He was sad, quiet, and he made love to her in a very different way—as if he needed to press himself inside her and stay there for a long time. When they were done he held her close to him and told her the story. He asked if she would come with him to his parents' apartment the following Sunday. It was too hard to go alone.

"Of course," she had said.

"I don't know who I am with them anymore," he said. "Since Thierry died. They need a good son."

She wondered if she was his attempt to fill that role.

But the following week he went to play a gig in Saint-Germain-en-Laye and he didn't come back. He texted her: *No lunch. Too trashed.*

So she was his good girl and he was her bad boy. Neither of them would change. He'd fuck his lead singer and she'd keep hoping for something like love.

She'd keep hoping for someone like Jeremy.

"May I join you?" a voice says in French, startling Chantal.

She looks up—it's Nico, with a radiant smile on his face.

"Of course," she says. Just seeing him lifts her heart.

He sits across from her; the smile has not left his face.

"You fell in love with your American French teacher," she says. She is surprised to feel disappointment, hard and real, pressing like a stone against her ribs.

"No. Yes," he says. He looks away and then places an envelope on the table between them. "This is for you."

He looks shy and boyish and she wonders if she'll have to hear all about the wonderful woman who captured his heart.

"Open it," he urges her.

She reaches for the envelope.

He reaches for her glass of wine, and their hands brush against each other. She feels the heat of him—that's what love does to a man, she thinks. She watches him take a sip of her wine. It's a remarkably intimate gesture. He hasn't even asked her if she minds. She follows the glass to his lips and for a moment his smile disappears and then it's there again, as if he's pleased she ordered this wine just for him.

"Champagne!" she says, remembering his promise to celebrate his book sale.

Nico gestures for the waiter, who appears at their table. He orders a bottle of champagne and two glasses. It seems that neither of them is waiting for Philippe to appear.

"Tell me about your book of poetry," Chantal says. She places her fingers on the envelope but doesn't open it.

"Just this morning I thought my poems were about shame," Nico says, and though his voice is serious, his face glows—he cannot contain his joy. "And now I think that's wrong. When I was a kid, I spent a day in a root cellar, hiding. I had fallen asleep there, and my parents thought I was lost or kidnapped or God knows what. When I woke up and saw the policemen searching for me, I stayed where I was, too scared to step back into the world. Over the past years I've written countless poems, reinventing what might have happened during that day."

"And none of them is true?" Chantal asks.

"They're all true," Nico says. "They all could have happened. They all continued to happen in my parents' imagination because I never told them where I was. I said I couldn't remember."

"Why?"

"Ah, there's the shame. But there's something else. I wanted a secret. I wanted something that was all mine, that no one could take away from me."

"And now? You're giving away your secret?"

"I don't need my secret anymore." Nico sits back in his chair. He keeps his eyes on Chantal.

"I don't understand," she says.

"That little boy in the root cellar is so lonely," Nico tells her. "I want something else."

"What do you want?"

"Open this," he says, touching her fingers, which rest on the envelope.

Chantal hears the young girl's new song, but this time the lyrics are in French. She sings about the language of love.

"Did you see the chanteuse?" Chantal asks Nico.

"She's a child," Nico says, nodding. "But if I close my eyes she's Édith Piaf."

"*Les mots d'amour*," Chantal repeats. "Sometimes at the end of a teaching day I feel like there are no words left."

"Did you say goodbye to your American?" Nico asks.

"Yes. This time I think the student taught the teacher more than the teacher taught the student."

The singer's voice rises and the conversations at the tables in the café all seem to pause for a moment.

He is part of my heart, the girls sings.

"What did you learn?" Nico asks.

"Oh, I learned that there's a kind of love which must feel like coming home," Chantal says, smiling. "It gives me a vision of what I'd like to have."

His eyes are on her, so she looks at the envelope. It's not sealed. She opens the flap and pulls out two tickets. It takes a few moments to make sense of them—theater tickets? Plane tickets? No, they're train tickets to Avignon. She furrows her brow but he doesn't say a word. She examines them more closely.

The train leaves at nine P.M. from Gare de Lyon.

"Say yes," Nico tells her.

She just looks at him.

"Can I have my wine back?"

He takes one more sip and passes it back to her. Again, their fingers touch.

"I thought I had fallen in love with the American, I really did," Nico says in a mad rush. "She was tragic and beautiful and I thought I'd save her. I invited her to Provence."

Why are you telling me this? Chantal thinks, but she doesn't say a word.

"She said she'd meet me at the train station. I got there early, and while I looked for her in the crowd I kept imagining your hair escaping from your bun, your eyes as they looked at me this morning, your graceful body walking through the crowd and appearing in front of me, ready to run away with me to Provence. I could smell summer—you smell like summer— I could feel your breath on my face. I'd shake the image away and tell myself no, that was nothing, that night we spent together. That was Chantal's revenge. I was waiting for Josie, not you, but the longer I waited the more I wanted *you* to appear, the more I wanted to climb onboard that train with you at my side. And the girl never showed, but if she had I would have told her I had made a terrible mistake—that she had made a terrible mistake—but she didn't appear, and I knew what I wanted."

He stops talking as suddenly as he began. She wonders for a moment if she's crazy or he's crazy. This might be a joke of sorts, something he and Philippe have created to make a fool of her.

Because she must be a fool—she's watching him with a smile on her face that she can't hide. She imagines the darkness of the train, the great speed, the closed space, the quiet hours. They would arrive at midnight, find a hotel, and hold each other through the night. In the morning there would be Provence— green, lush, ripe—and they could step out into this new world.

"I don't have clothes, toiletries," Chantal tells him, a little breathlessly.

"You don't need a thing. We'll spend the entire weekend naked in bed."

She smiles. "I'm the backup girl?"

"No," he says. He's quiet—it's as if he's run out of words. "I want *you,*" he finally says, his voice as hushed as a promise.

"I don't know what I want."

"You want Provence. We'll figure it out from there."

"Let's go," Chantal says, laughing.

Why not? she thinks. Why not look for love on a train from Paris to Provence. And in the morning, they'll wake in each other's arms, to greet the astonishing sun.

Acknowledgments

The writing process may be solitary, but the process of turning a manuscript into a published book takes a lot of help from my friends.

I'd like to thank my very smart readers: Neal Rothman, Lalita Tademy, Rosemary Graham, Elizabeth Stark, Amanda Eyre Ward, Allison Lynn, Meg Waite Clayton, Vicky Mlyniec, and Cornelia Read.

I owe a great deal to my remarkable agent, Sally Wofford-Girand.

I feel very lucky to have the talented Jennifer Smith as my editor. Gina Centrello, Libby McGuire, and Jane von Mehren, publishers extraordinaire, head up the Ballantine dream team. Sanyu Dillon was one of the first champions of *French Lessons* at Random House, and I greatly appreciate her unflagging support. A tip of the chapeau to Cindy Murray, my publicist, and to Kim Hovey and Leigh Marchant, who deserve a *coupe de cham-*

pagne and many, many thanks for their support and hard work. *Bisous* to all of you. The publishing process has never been so much fun.

Ilsa Brink designed my website—Ilsa, you're brilliant.

I am part of a wonderful women writers' community in the San Francisco Bay area: WOMBA (Word of Mouth–Bay Area). Thank you, Wombistas, for all your support along the way.

My fabulous students always inspire me. I'll share champagne with all of you.

Thank you, Daniela De Luca, my very dear friend, for the use of your fabulous apartment in Paris.

I have spent blissful writing weeks at Ledig House, Ragdale, Ucross, and Atlantic Center for the Arts—I am so grateful for what those residencies have given me.

Thanks to my friend Gary Lee Kraut, travel consultant and founder of FranceRevisited.com, who checked the manuscript for any mistakes in French or in my portrayal of Paris.

As always, my undying love and gratitude to Neal.

Indulge
in your own *Parisian* experience

To celebrate the publication of *French Lessons*

we're offering one lucky reader the chance to experience the romance of Paris for themselves with a luxurious weekend break.

The prize for two includes:

RETURN FLIGHTS OR EUROSTAR AND TRANSFERS

VIP AIRPORT LOUNGE OR CHAMPAGNE IF GOING BY EUROSTAR

2 NIGHTS 4* HOTEL ACCOMMODATION

DAILY BREAKFAST

SEINE RIVER CRUISE

HORSE AND CARRIAGE RIDE THROUGH PARIS

PARIS GUIDEBOOK

To be in with a chance of winning, go to our website:

www.canvasbooks.co.uk